LOST HORIZON

Also by Michael Ford

Forgotten City

LOST HORIZON

MICHAEL FORD

HARPER
An Imprint of HarperCollins*Publishers*

Lost Horizon

 For information address HarperCollins Children's Books, a division of HarperCollins Publishers, 195 Broadway, New York, NY 10007.

www.harpercollinschildrens.com

Library of Congress Control Number: 2019944061

ISBN 978-0-06-269699-1

Typography by Michelle Taormina

Interior Art by Michelle Taormina

19 20 21 22 23 PC/LSCH 10 9 8 7 6 5 4 3 2 1

❖

First Edition

1

"THE RULES KEEP US *alive.*"

He'd heard it a hundred times, so why hadn't he listened? Why hadn't he stayed put like he was supposed to?

"Dad?" Kobi whispered. He cut a path through coarse grass as tall as his shoulders, using his machete, then climbed a tangle of roots twisting out from the enormous trunk of a cedar. His eyes darted around the mutated undergrowth, searching for movement or for a sign his father might have come this way. There was nothing.

"I scout ahead; you stay exactly where you are until I come back and give you a signal. It's how we move safely. Got it?"

Kobi had begged his dad to take him along, to let Kobi go with him out into the Wastelands, train him how to survive. "I'm nine years old, Dad," he'd said. "I'm ready."

He'd been so stupid.

Kobi raised an arm to push through a curtain of leafy vines.

"Examine everything. Never move without looking."

Kobi froze.

Tiny serrated teeth edged along the lengths of the vines. The Waste had mutated them into flesh-eaters, Kobi realized. He peered up. High among the branches, a massive gull was trussed up inside a crisscrossing prison of tendrils. Acid sap dripped slowly over the carcass, dissolving it one feather at a time. Kobi saw a rib cage, melted flesh, a gleaming eyeball. He remembered what his dad had said: the ivy Chokerplants weren't as deadly as the ones that lashed out from underground, but if they got you they killed you a lot slower.

Trembling, Kobi crouched beneath the Choker. He glanced up at the sharp-bladed feelers, inches from brushing his back. He stumbled.

"Never rush, Kobi!"

Kobi screwed his eyes shut for a moment. His heart pounded like a drum in his ears, and he worried the feelers would sense the tremors.

After a minute, he moved off again, taking each step with careful precision, until he was finally out of the Choker's reach. "Dad?" Kobi called out as loud as he dared. "Where are you?"

He wanted to shout, to scream so his dad would hear him. But that would be suicide. Anything might hear. Chokers, wasps, wolves, bears, eagles.

Snatchers.

His dad had said the drones could pick up audio from five miles away.

Kobi bit his lip to stop himself whimpering. He was lost. Alone.

"Out here we're prey, Kobi. Remember that. There are a hundred things that can kill us."

It had been going so well, their first training session. But Kobi had gotten scared. When his father hadn't returned after ten minutes, he'd rushed after him. Betrayed his trust. That was the worst thing—worse even than the ball of fear building in his gut now. *I've let Dad down.*

He heard a noise, to his left. Just a rustle.

"Dad?"

He walked quickly, placing each foot with care on the spongy, moss-covered ground. He ducked under a branch, feeling twigs scrape at his hair. Sunlight trickled through a break in the foliage just ahead. The clearing where he was supposed to wait! He'd managed to circle back. He could wait here for his dad. Kobi wiped his tears away and hurried on. It was going to be okay. His dad might never know he hadn't waited.

Kobi burst through the veil of branches, tearing aside leaves bigger than his head.

His feet skidded in the mud as he stopped. It wasn't the clearing at all. It was a rocky wharf.

He gazed out over the largest expanse of water he'd ever seen—stretching out for miles.

"Elliott Bay," Kobi whispered. He'd seen it on maps. His breath shuddered in his chest at the size of it.

Huge patches of phosphorescence shimmered like spilled oil, and lily pads several feet across floated on the surface, sprouting flowers of every hue. Shreds of dense mist drifted in places, hovering over the surface. In the distance, on what must have been the far shore, colossal green monoliths soared into the clouds. *Downtown Seattle.* Bill Gates High School, where Kobi and his dad had made their base, was in West Seattle, a formerly residential area of the city. Unlike his dad, he'd never crossed the bridge to the downtown area, but he'd heard it was once home to two million people, before the Waste had wiped out the population and the genetically modified vegetation and animals had taken over.

Kobi was about to retreat from the bay and continue searching for his dad when his ears caught a sound: the soft slap of water. Then ripples began to pulse from a patch of mist, furrowing the surface until they reached the bank near his feet. When Kobi squinted, he could just make out a dark shape in the center of the lake, moving steadily parallel to the shore. His knees almost buckled as he took a slight sudden step forward. *A sail? A boat!*

His dad had always been so sure there were no other survivors, and if by a slim chance they *were* out there, they would be too hard to reach. But Kobi had always hoped. He could never get rid of the thought, a lingering, impossible dream that one day they might find others like them—kids his age, other families, people who they could rely on. And now, almost like a miracle, that day had really come. Here they were: survivors, just a few hundred yards away. Kobi found his voice. "Hey!" he called.

The boat kept going, drifting away into the mist.

"No! Wait!" Kobi shouted, waving his arms.

But the ship maintained its course, becoming a ghostly shape in the mist before disappearing entirely from view.

Kobi looked around for something to throw—a rock or a branch. Anything to get their attention. But there was nothing. He watched the mist again, pleading in his heart for them to turn around and come back. How could they not have heard him?

"Kobi!" called a distant, frantic voice. *Dad.* "Kobi, where are you?"

His eyes still on the water, Kobi shouted back. "I'm fine! I'm by the water. Dad, I—"

A vast gleaming fin sliced up from the depths, twenty yards out, and the surface ballooned upward as a massive body followed. Kobi staggered back.

What he'd seen, he realized, hadn't been a boat at all. A wall of water overwhelmed the bank and crashed over him, freezing and sudden. The ground turned to slick mud, and his feet slipped out from beneath him. Kobi felt the current snatch him up and suck his legs into the shallows. He twisted and clawed at the bank, but his fingers slid over the ground. And then he was under.

Kobi flailed. Water burned up his nostrils and into the back of his throat. He scrambled for purchase, but the bank dropped away suddenly. The churning water dragged him deeper. He couldn't swim. He couldn't breathe. But rearing above both of those fears was a greater terror: the creature looming out there in the murky water. His fingers brushed something slimy, and he recoiled, kicking out and striking a harder surface. A low, mournful sound—an eerie call—seemed to come from every direction at once. It was impossible to pinpoint. He felt the water stir again below, and looking down into the depths, he saw a flash of silver flesh, rolling, then a sickly yellow eye, watching him. It rolled back in a fleshy red socket, and the creature rose. The scale of its body seemed impossible. Frozen, Kobi took in the scarred flesh of its head, a blunt nose, a mouth that stretched open like a crack in the ground. Rows of jagged teeth, each curved fang long enough to pierce right through Kobi's body. . . .

Something clamped his upper arm, digging into the flesh, and pulled. Suddenly he was out of the water, being hauled to shore, slithering across the muddy bank. The water exploded upward, drenching him in its spray as a black-and-white body rose, then crashed down again. It was some sort of orca, Kobi realized, its skin gouged with scars and patches of red, raw flesh. Kobi watched it disappear beneath the surface as he was dragged farther from the water's edge.

His dad was here, hands clamped on Kobi's shoulders, pulling him to his feet. His eyes searched Kobi's body frantically.

"Are you hurt? Did it bite you?" he was saying.

"I . . . No . . . I'm fine," Kobi managed to reply.

His dad crouched in front of him, a look of utter panic on his face. "What the hell were you doing, son?"

"I . . . I thought it was a boat. Survivors."

His dad looked incredulous, shaking his head. Then he pulled Kobi into an embrace and held him firm. Kobi could feel his father's heart rattling.

"Never run off again," he said, squeezing more tightly. "Got it?"

"Got it," said Kobi.

His dad released him, staring hard and angry until Kobi couldn't maintain eye contact. His face flushing red, he glanced down.

"Look at me, Kobi," said his dad.

Kobi raised his gaze. His dad's face wasn't furious anymore. It was resigned. Sad, even.

"Son, there aren't any survivors," he said. He pointed at the city skyline across the bay. "I've been there. I've seen it. There's no one."

"But *we* survived," said Kobi. "Maybe there are others. If they had a home and could get food like us—"

"There *aren't*," said his dad. "Trust me. Even if the predators didn't get you over there the Waste would. There's no medicine. The air is toxic. A human wouldn't last a week."

Together they watched the surface of the lake for a few seconds. It was completely still again, with no clue of the horror that lurked within. Kobi wondered if he'd ever get chance to go into the city. Probably not, after today.

"Come on," said his dad. "Let's get back to base."

He stood, and helped Kobi to his feet as well, then folded an arm over Kobi's shoulders. "I thought I'd lost you," he said quietly, then sucked in a breath as if trying not to choke up. "I thought I lost you, son."

Kobi reached up and touched the rough skin of his father's hand on his shoulder, sliding his fingers through his dad's. They felt real, but he knew they weren't, and that made his heart ache too much to bear.

Kobi awoke from the dream. Though it wasn't a dream. It was more than that. A memory. A flashback. Kobi had been having them often. Like his past invaded the present whenever he was most vulnerable. He pushed his legs out from under the sheets and sat up, visions of the Wastelands still around him, cast against the gray concrete walls of his bedroom. There was no natural light, only a blue night-light. Kobi didn't like much other decoration. A few books, a couple of posters of his favorite movies he used to watch with Hales—classic black-and-white ones from almost a hundred years ago. Hales had liked those the best. Kobi realized his cheeks were moist, and he brushed the tracks away with his pajama sleeve.

"I thought I'd lost you. I thought I lost you, son."

Hales's words echoed again in Kobi's foggy brain, causing him a spasm of hurt. "I was never your son," he replied out loud.

"Kobi? You awake?" There was a knock at the door. Kobi wasn't allowed a lock, and before he could say anything the steel door swung open. It revealed Asha, watching him with dark eyes filled with worry. Her thick, black hair was hanging to her shoulders, bunching at the collar of a beige fleece and drifting in the air over her scalp, from the static, Kobi guessed, of putting on the sweatshirt. In the blue lamplight, her brown skin shone the color of dusk.

"I sensed you," she said. She tapped her temple. "This dream was really vivid."

Kobi just nodded. Asha was a Receptor, a telepath who could sense the thoughts and emotions of all organisms contaminated by the Waste. Without waiting for an invitation, she strolled in and sat beside him. "You saw an orca? That's what that thing was in the bay."

"Yes," said Kobi. He cleared his throat. "That was my first day training outside the school with Hales. After that we didn't go out again for months. I still don't like water—the ocean or lakes or anything. Not many of those around here." He smiled at her.

She returned the smile for a second before looking away, wistful. "I'd like to see the ocean one day. We never saw it when we were with you in the Wastelands."

"I guess there wasn't much time for sightseeing."

She sat down on the bed. Kobi didn't need Asha's telepathic powers to read the guilt on her face. "Not really," she said. "But that's the past now. We need to focus on the future."

Like Kobi, Asha had grown up believing human society had been completely destroyed by the Waste after it was released into the environment over twenty years ago—the chemical that had been intended to accelerate the growth of crops but had instead spread through the environment, mutating plants and animals and killing humans. Until six months ago, she'd lived her whole life in a secure facility called Healhome. The scientists there, led by Melanie Garcia and calling themselves "Guardians," had told Asha and the other kids that they had a natural resistance to the Waste. They said they were studying the kids' resistance to find a cure. But it was all lies.

The truth was, only pockets of the world had been ruined by the Waste. Those had been cordoned off in quarantine zones; the rest of the world was intact. Healhome was really hidden away at the top of a skyscraper in the city of New Seattle—a hundred miles from the city now called *Old* Seattle, built as a symbol of humanity's defiance against the Waste. Melanie had told the truth about one thing: she was CEO of CLAWS—the Corporation of Leading Anti-Waste Scientists. But they weren't trying to find a cure. They just wanted their drugs to work well enough that the people of New Seattle would keep coming back for more. CLAWS had been experimenting on human embryos, contaminating them with Waste on purpose. Most died, but some survived, the Waste's mutations giving them strange, superhuman abilities.

Kobi had been one of those embryos too, and the only one to develop complete Waste immunity. So when he was a baby, Dr. Jonathan Hales, a CLAWS scientist, had kidnapped him and taken him to Old Seattle, the heart of the Wastelands. He'd thought they would be safe there, long enough for Hales to develop from Kobi's blood a *real* cure for the Waste. Hales knew that if CLAWS realized Kobi was entirely immune, they would kill him rather than see their empire threatened. Hales told Kobi he was his father so Kobi would never question anything he said.

Six months ago, CLAWS had dispatched Asha and two other Healhome kids to the Wastelands to find Kobi—an eleven-year-old boy called Fionn and Niki, who was fourteen like Asha, a year older than Kobi. After finding Kobi's dad's secret lab, Asha had called in reinforcements from CLAWS. Kobi didn't blame her anymore—she had been manipulated. But Asha still found any mention of it awkward.

"Sorry. I don't always mean to listen in on your dreams, you know," Asha said. "I can't control my powers when I'm sleeping. It's not actually fun to live other people's nightmares."

Kobi nodded. "Right. You don't have to apologize."

"Have you told Mischik about this memory?" She pointed to the journal on his desk, where Kobi had been ordered to write down anything he remembered about Hales's work. Next to it lay a map of Old Seattle that Kobi had labeled with all of Hales's labs and supply caches.

"I've told Mischik about everything, just like he asked. But he doesn't seem that interested."

"He just wants you to keep focused on the plan," said Asha, echoing what Mischik had repeated over and over to Kobi.

Right. The plan. The one that means I'm stuck waiting around here.

He'd thought that joining the resistance against CLAWS

would mean *doing* something. But so far all he'd done was wait.

Kobi stood up and moved to his small wardrobe. "Let's head to the game room. I need to . . . *do* something. Blow off some steam."

Asha watched him. "I know you're frustrated, Kobi. I'm sure this place is pretty claustrophobic to you, coming from your old life outside. But we have to stay strong."

"I know," Kobi grumbled. The longer he stayed in this base, the less *strong* he felt: his body felt tired, his mind foggy. "I need to get changed."

"I'll wait outside," Asha said.

As soon as the door shut behind her, Kobi sighed. He couldn't go anywhere without someone accompanying him. It felt like he was being watched every second of the day.

And he was. In the corner of the bedroom, the small red light of a camera blinked. "We can't risk anything happening to you, Kobi," Mischik had said. "We need to keep an eye on you. Just in case."

Kobi changed and left the room, brushing past Asha to lead the way through the base. Hales had taught him to imprint safe routes into his memory; it meant he could navigate the maze of tunnels toward the game room without thinking. Kobi heard the gushing of running water above him, and for a moment he felt himself transported back beneath the lake: the current rushing in his ears, drowning his scream, heavy clothes pulling him down, a giant yellow eye watching him through the murky depths. His step ceased, his boot making a heavy clang on the metal floor.

"You okay?" Asha asked. Kobi felt his head prickling as Asha read his mind.

Kobi squeezed his fists. "Yeah, it's just the water pipes."

Asha looked up. This facility had once housed machinery for generating, storing, and transmitting hydroelectric power from the nearby Columbia River dams, before the tech was made obsolete by the biofuel plants of CLAWS. But the underground tunnels had never been removed. There were enough secret access shafts that Sol's resistance fighters could stay hidden but also move around the city, like rabbits in a warren, out of sight of CLAWS and the New Seattle authorities.

A few Sol scientists wearing lab coats paused to watch him, muttering. Maybe with excitement or maybe with worry. Kobi knew their work wasn't going well—synthesizing his antibodies to increase production of their new anti-Waste cleanser, a drug they'd called Horizon.

When they reached the main set of corridors, Kobi pressed his thumb onto the scanner, and the doors slid apart in a hiss of air, revealing a large central atrium space with corridors and gangways leading off it at various heights. Metal mesh stairs climbed up to the different levels, encircling the space like an amphitheater, or a prison. There were scientists, tech guys, and Sol field agents everywhere here—perhaps a hundred altogether, striding back and forth between meeting rooms, weaponry stores, and labs. They watched Kobi with awed faces as he passed.

"If it isn't our savior!" Kobi turned to a young man with straggly hair and thick hexagonal glasses. He was eating a giant baloney sandwich. Some of the filling had fallen down the front of his shaggy Metallica T-shirt.

"Hey, Spike," said Kobi with a grin.

He caught a flicker of movement just behind him. He turned and found Asha shaking her head insistently at Spike.

"Uh, or not-savior," Spike said.

"Don't worry," said Kobi, rolling his eyes. "Asha just wants to take the pressure off me as much as possible." Kobi lowered his voice. "Affects my production of antibodies."

"Hey, that's not the reason," Asha protested.

Spike gave a toothy smile. "Hey, we're all stressed." He pulled out a small metal object from his jeans pocket and threw it into the air. It uncoiled into the shape of a metallic insect, which began to hover in the air on a blur of buzzing wings. "I'm about to show off this new hacker bug to the bigwigs."

"Cool!" said Kobi. Spike had been helping Kobi catch up with modern technology—VR goggles, holo-tech, drones—taking apart machinery and showing him how it worked. It helped Kobi relax, like he was back helping Hales in his workshop.

"We call it the dragonfly," said Spike. "It locks on to drones and hacks into the CLAWS comms network. We'll get the lowdown on their plans—plus we might even be able to use their drones to send our own messages to everyone with a CLAWS app on their device. Which is basically everyone in the world. The signal won't get blocked if it originates from CLAWS tech. We'll finally be able to get the truth out there. Neat, huh?"

"You're a genius, Spike," Kobi agreed, grinning.

"You said it." Spike took a bite of the sandwich but almost spit it out again as he caught sight of something over Kobi's shoulder. "Sorry, gotta go. Boss is here." A cluster of important-looking adults was pacing through the atrium, including the tall figure of Alex Mischik, leader of Sol. Spike quickly grabbed the dragonfly from the air and stuffed it in his pocket. "Probably shouldn't be showing this thing around just yet." He slapped Kobi on the shoulder. "See you—savior." He grinned at Asha, who shook her head, letting out a disapproving sigh.

"You've got to give Spike a break," said Kobi as they walked away. "At least he doesn't treat me like some kind of prophet, or like I'm going to fall apart if people come near me."

"People just want you to be focused," Asha told him again. "They stay away so they don't distract you."

Kobi didn't reply. He'd been focused on supplying his blood to make the Horizon drugs for going on six months now, and it didn't feel like Sol was any closer to breaking the stranglehold CLAWS had on the city.

"We have to have faith," said Asha. "Put our own discomfort aside for the greater good. I'm sorry, Kobi. I know it's frustrating, but soon we *will* win. One day CLAWS, the Waste—all of it will be gone. Things will be like they were before the Waste disaster."

Kobi listened to her, trying to picture it: being a normal kid, going to school, hanging out with friends. Having a family. Where would he live? With Mischik or the other Healhome kids? Would someone adopt them?

The only thing he could come up with seemed cheesy and fake—like a commercial. A laughing family sitting around a dinner table in a neat kitchen. The real problem was that every time Kobi tried to imagine the future, the past invaded, and one face was stranded there forever: Jonathan Hales. The only family Kobi had ever known.

2

KOBI AND ASHA FINALLY reached the game room after another ten minutes navigating the base's labyrinthine underbelly. Kobi practically ran through the wide archway into the old turbine hall. The ceiling was leaking, and the air smelled musty and damp. When they'd first arrived at the Sol base, the kids had tacked posters up on the bare concrete walls and moved the pieces of old gym equipment into one corner. There were a basketball hoop, a pool table, and a few sofas, where Leon and Rohan were currently lounging. Mischik had wanted a space where Kobi and the Healhome kids could relax.

Kobi nodded to Leon and Rohan, then went straight to the pull-up bars, where he started a set of muscle-ups: he pulled his chin to the level of the bar, then pushed his body up over it, locking his arms, then lowered himself back down to repeat the exercise. His arms began to shake after twenty reps, but Kobi felt good.

Finally, the lingering fear and grief from his dream began to fade.

Asha flopped down onto a beanbag and got out the new smartphone Sol had given her. A series of holo apps projected into the air. Many of the apps were CLAWS apps: the Waste Level Monitoring app, CLAWS News, Waste Scanner, CLAWS Groceries. Asha liked to keep tabs on what CLAWS was up to. She pointed her finger into the floating holo-image of the Waste Level Monitoring app, which opened with the CLAWS logo. It showed a live feed of the city, filmed from a drone hundreds of feet above. A yellow-and-orange overlay showed the different levels of Waste across the city. Most of the slums were covered in red. The app read: *Waste levels in your area critical. Stay inside.*

"Nothing new there, then," said Kobi, stepping on the bar and gripping it with his bare feet. He somersaulted off but stumbled as he landed, a stab of pain jarring up his knee. He gritted his teeth, mostly in irritation; he was better than that.

"There's a video alert," said Asha. She poked at the icon of a camera, and Sam Stone, the morning anchor on the CLAWS news station, appeared.

"Cases of Waste contamination are up two point three percent, with sharp increases in the outlying districts. Movement between containment zones is strictly prohibited. Lawbreakers face immediate removal by extraction drone. Brett Johns, Chief Science Officer at CLAWS, says the rise is, quote, not a cause for concern if people follow the rules and stick to their anti-Waste pharma programs, unquote."

"Hey, Caveman—heads up!"

Kobi spun around just in time to see Leon hurl a baseball from the other side of the room. Not accurately but fast. Kobi flung himself after it but missed, and the ball shot through the hologram, distorting Sam Stone's face for a moment before bouncing off the wall. Kobi picked it up.

"You're not going to make the Sol team unless you sharpen up," said Leon, flicking the long hair from his eyes. Leon was another Healhome kid, tall and wiry like a rock climber. His usual mischievous grin creased his long bony face.

"Hey, I was close," said Kobi, tossing the ball up and down in his hand. "And you know I'd be the best pitcher. You can't throw straight." He launched the ball back as hard as he could toward Leon. But he dragged the throw, and the ball swerved toward Rohan, who was still sitting on a couch, reading on a tablet.

"Heads up!" yelled Leon.

Rohan glanced up and snatched the ball from the air with one hand. "You're out!" he said. Rohan's eyes were yellow, almost gold, shining out from a warm face with compact features. His skin was light brown and his hair a deep glossy black, falling just to above his ears. His vision had been enhanced by Waste on many levels: he could see perfectly in the dark, detect heat and cold sources on the infrared spectrum, and even pick out Waste visually. His mutation also gave him the power to process even the fastest kinetic movements in a thousandth of a second—he described it like seeing the whole world in super slow motion.

"Told you Caveman can't play baseball," Leon complained. "That's what happens when you grow up in the wild."

Kobi shook his head with a smile, not rising to Leon's baiting. He appreciated Leon and Rohan not treating him like he was some precious resource that had to be protected. When he was around them, he could almost imagine he really was a normal kid. Almost.

"Am I on the team, then?" Rohan asked, holding up the ball. "You need fielders, right?"

"You're banned, sadly," said Leon. "I told one of the lab guys about you, and they said you had an unfair advantage."

"Says the guy whose muscles can generate five times the power of a normal person," said Rohan with a snort, returning to his magazine. "This is discrimination, pure and simple."

"Fine, you're in. But *I'm* pitcher." Leon threw the ball back to Kobi, and this time Kobi jumped high and caught it. The Waste had given him enhanced strength, speed, and healing—abilities Jonathan Hales had tested regularly back at their base in Old Seattle. These were baseline abilities caused by all Waste mutations. Every Healhome kid had them to some degree. But Johanna, the older Healhome girl with barklike skin, had told Kobi his baseline abilities were stronger than the others. His healing ability in particular.

"Hey, have you seen any sign of Fionn?" said Asha, coming over. She was trying to make herself sound casual, but her hands fidgeted nervously at her sides. The others looked at one another. None of them had seen Fionn in a week. It wasn't like he was missing or anything—just off exploring the network of tunnels under the base, which extended for miles underground. Asha had told them she'd sensed him coming back to his dorm to sleep, and Johanna said he'd been turning up for occasional testing, but he'd always slip away before any of the others could see him. No one wanted to tell Mischik in case they got Fionn in trouble. But as the days passed, like Asha, Kobi felt increasingly worried.

"He can handle himself," Kobi said, as much to convince himself as Asha.

"Can't you sense him now?" Leon asked. "Check if he's okay?"

Asha bit her lip and looked down. "Not today. It's like he's blocking me out. All I get when I try to sense his thoughts is just . . . blankness." She tapped her watch communicator. "He's not answering calls either."

"Maybe he just wants some privacy," Leon said. "Where's he even gonna go?"

"I guess," said Asha, but Kobi could see she was troubled.

"I saw him," said a voice above. Kobi looked up and saw Yaeko hanging from the steel mesh of the industrial pipes lining the ceiling. Her skin shimmered a dull silver. As with many of the Healhome kids, she was a "blend": animal DNA—in her case that of a chameleon—had found its way into her DNA in the sample of Waste CLAWS had used on her while she was still an embryo. The exotic lizard must have been kept as a pet in the city and escaped, its body decomposing into the ecosystem. At least that was the theory. Johanna thought it unlikely. She believed that the animal

DNA had been added intentionally by CLAWS. Perhaps they believed it might help the kids develop immunity, or maybe they were just experimenting out of twisted curiosity. Kobi wouldn't put it past them.

Asha crossed her arms. "You going to tell me where, Yaeko, or you just going to hang there?"

In a blink, Yaeko vanished. Kobi spotted movement on the ceiling and tracked Yaeko crawling over to the seating area a few seconds later. He could make out only the rough shape of her black T-shirt and jean shorts.

Asha sighed with frustration. "Yaeko! You want me to beg? Just tell me."

Yaeko flashed back into view. She looked at her nails, didn't say anything, then eventually shrugged. "If you really want to know, I caught him sneaking away with some food from the cafeteria. I followed him through some of the deep tunnels that Sol doesn't use, then he went down this old padlocked manhole. Must have broken it open. There was a danger sign on the cover." She smiled sweetly at Asha. "I didn't feel like following anymore. *I* got the hint." Asha ground her jaw. No one could rile her up like Yaeko, and Fionn was one subject she was always touchy on.

"Ignore her," said Rohan.

"We can check out the tunnel if you want," said Kobi. "But I think it's better to let Fionn come to us when he's ready."

Asha glowered at each of them in turn. "Fine," she muttered.

On Kobi's wrist, his watch communicator vibrated. An

incoming call. He answered, and a small hologram of Alex Mischik's head popped up.

"Time to draw blood, Kobi," said the head of Sol.

"Again?" Kobi asked.

"Sector G," said Mischik. "Room four." He disappeared.

"Better hurry, Caveman," said Leon. "Don't want to keep the boss waiting!"

Kobi watched the needle slide into the catheter in his forearm, connected to a translucent tube that began to fill with dark blood. The tube led to an empty blood bag among a few already filled bags hanging from a cart. The vine-like tendrils of Johanna's fingers slithered through the air and wrapped around the bag, like mini-Chokerplants, as she tilted it to check if it was filling correctly.

"Just one more bag to go," she said to Kobi as the woody tendrils shriveled back, stiffening into fingers and a thumb. Kobi liked Johanna, but her mutation gave him the creeps. The Sol scientists guessed Choker and tree DNA had entered her body with the Waste, turning her skin the texture of bark and giving her hands and arms the ability to whip into long plantlike tendrils with remarkable dexterity.

"Is that all?" said Kobi. He hadn't meant for it to come out sarcastic, but Johanna frowned at him.

"Sorry, Kobi—it should be only another five minutes with the rate your heart can pump it out."

"It took longer than that last time," he replied.

Johanna pushed herself away on a rolling chair. Sometimes he wished that their roles were reversed. He could be working in the lab, and she could take his position.

Kobi gritted his teeth as blood streaked from his arm, opening and closing his hand to increase the flow.

"Getting there," Johanna said.

Kobi nodded, ignoring the pain. This was the problem with his Waste-given healing abilities. The skin broken by the needle kept trying to repair itself. The catheter—a small plastic device left under his skin and connected to his veins—had been fitted so there would be less tissue to pierce, but still, prolonged blood-drawing sessions twice a day took their toll.

The door opened, and Mischik himself entered the treatment room. He had salt-and-pepper hair, blue eyes, and a slightly grizzled complexion. Unremarkable—if not for the fact that his face appeared on Wanted posters across the city, proclaiming him a terrorist and a threat to society.

"How are things going here?" he asked.

Johanna glanced at the monitor relaying Kobi's blood pressure. "We're a little short," she said. "It looks like Kobi's blood isn't replenishing at the increased rate we expected." She removed the needle, pulling at the skin that had formed around it until the skin broke. Kobi grunted at the tearing sensation. Johanna used a cotton pad to dab up a small bead of blood; all that had escaped before the cut had healed.

"Is that a problem?" asked Kobi.

Mischik inspected the hanging bags and frowned. "Probably not," he said. "It's just I'd expected your body to adapt to the de-sanguination procedure by metabolizing more blood more quickly." He looked at Johanna. "Can we get in another session tonight?"

"You're already taking four pints a day!" Kobi burst out. He was annoyed the question was being addressed to Johanna, as if it was *her* blood they were taking.

Johanna shook her head. "Not at this stage," she said. "It would compromise Kobi's overall health."

Mischik folded his arms. "That's a shame," he muttered as if to himself.

"Sorry I'm such a disappointment," Kobi said.

Mischik smiled, but his eyes remained steely. "It's not your fault, Kobi," he said. It seemed he'd completely missed the sarcasm. "It's just we promised we'd start shipping Waste cleansers to a few clinics in other cities." He gave Kobi a playful slap on the shoulder. "You're in demand, kid."

So everyone keeps telling me, thought Kobi.

"Just lie still a few more minutes," said Johanna.

He watched Mischik loading the bags of blood into a cold storage pack. He wasn't sure exactly what happened to it now, other than a filtering process to isolate the anti-Waste antibodies and then activate them with a precise concentration of Waste—a process perfected over years by Jonathan Hales in Old Seattle. Then it would be apportioned into the Horizon cleansers.

"Any progress on synthesizing new antibodies?" Kobi asked. If Sol's scientists found a way to create antibodies in the lab, they wouldn't even need to draw blood from him.

Mischik shook his head. "We thought we were close to cracking it, but the latest batch of tests came back negative."

He sounded beat down. It made sense. They could really help only a limited number of people if Kobi was their only source of antibodies, so CLAWS would maintain their stranglehold on the drug market.

We should be out there, Kobi thought. With Yaeko's camouflage, Leon's strength . . . *We should be taking down CLAWS right now*. As Mischik began heading for the door, Kobi spoke up.

"You know, maybe we could help."

Mischik paused. "Help how?"

Kobi had rehearsed this speech dozens of times over the past six weeks, but now that the moment was here, the words just came tumbling out.

"With the fight against CLAWS," he said. "I mean, we're just sitting around down here. We've got abilities . . . powers. . . . We could—"

"You're children," said Mischik. Kobi saw Johanna's expression harden beneath her barklike skin, and the Sol leader must have seen it too. "I'm not being dismissive of your powers," he added. "You're all remarkably gifted. What I mean is that I'm not going to risk your lives. Especially not without a cast-iron strategy. We're not terrorists trying to cause chaos and fear, despite what Melanie Garcia is saying. If we go down the path of violence, we will only prove them right. Planting bombs, carrying out sabotage missions—it wouldn't get us anywhere. CLAWS is too powerful. We need to be smarter than them, and at the moment that means focusing on distributing Horizon. If enough people start using it and see its effects, they'll realize CLAWS has been cheating them. We'll win hearts and minds, and that's the beginning of a *true*, sustainable uprising."

Kobi found himself nodding, caught up in Mischik's inspiring words. He was right—but the little ice-box in his hands looked more pathetic than ever. Could they really win hearts and minds with four pints of blood a day?

There's another way, Kobi thought, thinking of the pages in his journal. The labs Hales had left behind, out in the Wastelands.

"What about Hales's research?" he said. Mischik's eyes narrowed; he had to know exactly what Kobi was talking about. In the former GrowCycle Lab in Old Seattle, where Hales had carried out most of his research, Kobi had found two folders. The first, labeled *1.3*, described testing on a chemical that sounded exactly like Waste. The second had been marked with *2.0* and his dad's scrawled notes: *Other Testing. Full Cure, Part Two. Send to Alex.*

"The notes he left on that folder—the folder marked 2.0—about a full cure and other testing, in the old GrowCycle Lab," Kobi told Mischik. "There must be something there we can use.

Hales wouldn't have written that for nothing. Maybe he already found the way to make a permanent cure. Something that will do more than just temporarily cleanse the Waste until you're exposed again."

Mischik watched him coolly. His pale eyes gave nothing away, but Kobi sensed a hardness behind them, a resoluteness that wouldn't budge.

Kobi's voice faltered slightly. "So . . . think about it. . . . With a full cure you would need only one dose. It would be so much cheaper and faster to spread the drugs. And . . . we wouldn't have to live in fear anymore. That's how CLAWS stays in control. The fear of Waste coming back. But if everyone was immune—*cured*—that fear would be shattered."

Mischik frowned, taking in Kobi's words before turning his head away slightly. "Hales was an optimist."

"If he thought the cleansers would be enough to defeat CLAWS, he would have come back from the Wastelands ages ago. He'd been using cleansers on himself for years, hadn't he?" Mischik's jaw clenched, but Kobi continued before the man could say anything. "Who better to go and find this cure than me—than the other mutated kids? We're adapted for survival in the Wastelands. There were loads of labs marked on his map. I think I've remembered them all. We just need to go through them one by one."

"CLAWS will have cleaned out the GrowCycle Lab," said Mischik. "And they took Hales's map, so they know the locations of the other labs too."

Kobi shook his head. "I know my dad!" He paused, realizing his slip. "Hales, I mean. He would have been prepared. He would have had backups. He would have spread his research out. If he wanted to keep something hidden, it would stay hidden."

They locked eyes, and Kobi knew they were thinking the same thing. Hales had kept Kobi hidden all those years. Through lying and manipulation. *Except they found us eventually. Maybe CLAWS* has *already gotten their hands on the research. But I have to try.*

From Mischik's softening gaze, Kobi could see he was wavering, tempted by the possibilities Kobi was suggesting. A real, *permanent* solution to the Waste—one that would destroy CLAWS.

"I agree with Kobi," said Johanna quietly. "I don't know if we can win this battle with a limited supply of blood. I don't know if you've seen the news, but Waste contamination is getting worse in the city. Even if we had enough cleansers for everyone, people will only get reinfected."

Mischik sighed and bent down to place the cooler on the floor. He rubbed his eyes as if suddenly weary.

"We might not win," he said, "but for the first time in forever we're not losing. Kobi—I can't risk it. If we lose you, we lose *everything.* Surely you can see that? We need you down here, safe. Our revolution has only just begun."

Kobi wasn't ready to let it go. "Maybe it's being down here that's stalling my progress," he said. "Back in the old city, I was improving all the time, in every metric. Strength, speed, regeneration. I think it's because Dad—Hales, I mean—he pushed me. I was . . .

useful. I was learning, fighting every day. Here, it feels like . . . I don't know . . . I'm going nowhere. Like I'm being suffocated."

"You have other kids like you," offered Mischik halfheartedly. "And the game room."

"Throwing a baseball, playing pool, and listening to Leon's movie rants are not the same," Kobi said. "I'm going crazy. We all are."

"Well, I don't know what to tell you," Mischik said. "If you think I'm going to authorize a suicide mission sending our most valuable asset into the Wastelands . . ."

Johanna cleared her throat and said softly, "Kobi's body could be failing to produce more antibodies because of this lack of stimulation."

Kobi turned back to Mischik, feeling a surge of triumph. "Let me prove it to you," he said. "That we can handle ourselves." An idea hit him. "Maybe we should start with something smaller. We could help with one of the Horizon deliveries?" Kobi had been allowed to sit in on some of the mission debriefs. It was just a case of visiting the clinics in the slums and dropping off the drugs.

"No," said Mischik. "Unnecessary risk."

"How many times have they even run into trouble?" Kobi asked, frustration building again. "I bet none."

"That's not the point!" Mischik said. He was almost shouting. "You're safest staying underground."

Kobi stood up to face him. "And what if I *won't* stay

underground? What if we decide to leave?" Mischik's race reddened. He could see Johanna looking anxious too. But Kobi persisted. "Look, I'm not saying we're going to run away—I don't think anyone wants that. But you have to let us do *something.* We're not asking to go out and have a party. Just a short journey, in an almost completely safe environment. I handled the Wastelands for thirteen years—where everything around me was trying to kill me. I can handle this city. I was raised to survive! It's what I'm good at!"

"There are CLAWS drones out there," said Mischik. "They'll be programmed to detect Waste contaminants—and that includes you, Kobi."

"We had Snatchers in the Wastelands. There are ways to hide. If anything goes wrong, we can abort the mission."

Mischik took a deep breath. "All right, Kobi. I'll discuss with the team."

"Is that a yes?" asked Kobi, grinning.

"It's a maybe," said Mischik. "You know, you're almost as stubborn as Jonathan was."

Like father like son, thought Kobi ironically. He wondered for a moment how much of Hales had been passed on to him. How much of his character. *I knew him better than anyone. I can't deny that. And I* know *this cure is out there. I just know.* He felt a rush of hope and excitement like he hadn't experienced in a long time. *All we have to do is prove ourselves on this mission and I know we can convince Mischik to let us go back to Old Seattle.*

"I'll tell the others," Kobi said.

Mischik flicked his eyes to the ceiling. "Don't make me regret this."

For a second, Kobi was reminded of his dream that morning; how he'd convinced Hales to let him go out on a mission before he was ready and the almost fatal consequences. He felt a shiver of doubt, but he squashed it quickly. That had been years ago.

I can do this. I'm ready.

3

TWO HOURS LATER, KOBI was gathered with Asha, Rohan, Leon, and Yaeko in a briefing room on C-Level, a dingy office space that had once been used by management at the hydroelectric plant. There were old, shabby, padded seats and a whiteboard. Old blueprints of the hydroelectric tunnel network remained visible where they'd been stenciled directly over the chipped paint of the walls. The hum of the strip lighting made Kobi uneasy; it reminded him of insects, a constant danger out in the Wastelands. A mutated wasp had once tried to nest in the school—that hadn't been fun. He tensed all his muscles. It was a technique the Sol psychiatrist had taught him to relieve anxiety: tense his whole body, then release each muscle. "Can we start already?" he said as he let his body relax, trying to ignore the humming.

Mischik was standing at the front of the room. Despite all the questions Rohan had fired at him since they sat down, the Sol leader was keeping quiet. He tapped his watch. "A few minutes. General Okafor always arrives precisely on time."

"General Okafor is running the briefing?" said Rohan excitedly.

"He is," said Mischik.

Rohan turned back from the row in front of Kobi and Asha. Leon was slumped next to him. "You know Okafor's story, right?"

"No, but something tells me you're going to tell us," said Leon. "Have you ever met a bigger gossip?" he said to Asha and Kobi. "You should see him getting the lowdown from the cafeteria staff."

Rohan grinned. "Denise and Frank are my best sources—they overhear everything. Just compliment their mac and cheese, and they pass on all their info. Missions, meetings, who's who in Sol, the code names of moles working at CLAWS: juicy stuff."

"Suck-up," said Leon, giving Rohan a playful shove.

Kobi felt a little jealous that Rohan could make friends with the Sol workers so easily. Except for Spike, of course.

"Go on, then. Get on with it," Yaeko called to Rohan from where she was lounging with her feet up in the back row, looking bored.

"Okafor led the rescue operation when the Waste first hit," Rohan said. "It was before anyone knew what they were dealing with. His para squad dropped right into the heart of the old city—people infected everywhere, animals already mutating and going *crazy*. He lost his legs to a mutant crocodile that escaped the Seattle zoo."

Asha leaned back in her chair, looking unconvinced. "Are you sure Denise and Frank weren't making that up?"

"They overheard some of the Sol agents talking," Rohan said. "And *I* heard from this Intel guy who likes the same comics as me that ten years ago, when Okafor was high up in the military, CLAWS tried to sell him what they called 'augmented bodily weaponry'—giving people superhuman abilities to create super soldiers. Remind you of anything?" He glanced pointedly around at the seated kids. "Anyway, Okafor took the story to the press. He didn't know that CLAWS already had people high up in the army and the government. They squashed the story and got him fired, and that's why he joined Sol."

Kobi shook his head. He hadn't been living in the real world long—if you could call this place the real world—but he was no longer surprised by the power and efficiency of the CLAWS PR machine. Every news channel he watched or newspaper he read was pro-CLAWS. They had the most powerful lobbyists in government. When your products were the only means to protect humanity against the Waste, you made a lot of friends and not many enemies.

Rohan continued. "Apparently, after he'd recovered from his legs being amputated, he led a bunch more missions into the Wastelands, looking for survivors. He even found the alligator and killed it. He's got a necklace made of its teeth!"

Kobi laughed. "Sounds like you've been reading too many of those comics."

"I thought you said it was a crocodile," Leon said.

Rohan raised his hands. "Crocodile, alligator . . . Who cares? The point is he's a hero."

"Well, thank you for the compliment," a voice rang out.

Everyone turned around as one. Mischik was chuckling as General Okafor wheeled himself into the room. He was a stocky man with a buzz cut. A faded pink scar cut across his temple, puckering the surrounding dark brown skin. One half of his face sagged a little, and his shoulder sloped sharply downward too. He wasn't wearing any prosthetics today; the stumps of his legs protruded from a pair of camouflage shorts.

"So what was it?" Leon asked Okafor. "An alligator?" Rohan looked embarrassed.

"No," said Okafor. Leon shot a triumphant look at Rohan. "It was the Waste. CLAWS was only in its infancy back then. There were no anti-Waste drugs when we first went in. We had only biohazard suits and masks. We weren't expecting the hostility of the mutated organisms. I lost a lot of good men and women, but the docs managed to save me. A contaminated ant bit through my suit, caught both legs. Painful, I can tell you. But they amputated the legs before the chemical spread too far through my body. Sorry to disappoint you." The room went quiet, then Okafor broke into the smallest of smiles. "And I don't wear necklaces."

"An *ant*?" said Rohan, mouth hanging open.

"Don't worry, they're scary enough," said Kobi, slapping Rohan on the shoulder. "Mandibles like samurai swords."

"Right," said Mischik. "We'd better get started. Where's Fionn?"

"We haven't seen him for a week," said Asha, concern spread across her face. "I wanted to tell you, actually. I've been able to sense him before, but I can't now—he's blocking me out."

Kobi raised his eyebrows. Fionn was a Projector, a type of telepath who could transmit his thoughts and emotions to plants and animals affected by Waste contamination. In the Wastelands, he had tamed a mutated wolf, held back a pack of flesh-eating rats, and even controlled a Chokerplant. Fionn had been mute since undergoing a traumatic CLAWS experiment when he was young, and now he only "talked" telepathically with Asha, whose Receptor abilities made her particularly astute at understanding Fionn's thoughts and emotions. If Fionn had found a way to prevent himself from being sensed telepathically by Asha, it was a step up in his powers. "He hasn't attended his testing today either," Johanna added. Kobi raised his head, feeling a clench of concern in his chest. What if Fionn had gotten injured or lost in the tunnels?

"The kid can't have gone far," said the general. "He doesn't have clearance for any of the exits."

"I suppose so," said Mischik. "Still, it's not good. I'll put together a search team to track him down." Knowing that Sol would be searching for Fionn made Kobi feel a little better.

"If you can't keep track of your people in here I'd say that bodes poorly for a mission outside," Okafor said.

A tiny flicker of annoyance passed across Mischik's face. But he nodded. "For what it's worth, I'm inclined to agree. Which is why I wanted you in charge. This will be a limited-scope, tightly controlled excursion. In and out, low risk."

"You got it, chief!" Rohan said, cutting through the tense exchange.

Mischik smiled, but Okafor still looked deadly serious. He placed a metal capsule on a long table at the front, and an image projected up from it in a widening beam of light. Okafor put his hands together in a prayerlike gesture before gradually pulling them apart, making the screen enlarge. It depicted an aerial shot of the New Seattle slums. Miles of ramshackle housing covered the mountainside, narrow streets winding between. Overlaid were several red circles.

"Listen up. What you see here are the various secret access points from the Sol base into the slums." He pointed a laser pen at the screen and clicked a button; a green cross appeared on the layout of the city. "And that's the clinic. The plan is to send an advance party—you—on foot. You'll be in disguise. Your job is to get to the clinic, confirm it's free of drones and CLAWS operatives, and then call in the delivery van with the Waste cleansers. If anything goes wrong—if there's anything even slightly suspicious—you call it off and we'll send in an extraction team. Understood?"

"Will we have time to do any sightseeing?" asked Rohan. Okafor and Mischik both fixed him with a stare. "Just kidding!" he added.

"This really isn't a time for jokes," Mischik said.

Okafor pointed to Kobi. "You'll be the point man up front. Leon and Rohan will follow and keep you out of harm's way."

"Like bodyguards," said Leon, turning back to Kobi. "We'll keep you safe."

"You'd better," retorted Kobi, but he was glad his friends seemed as excited as he was. He felt the same swell of hope as the one he'd experienced in the medical wing when Mischik had agreed to the mission. It was just like before, whenever he'd gone on a mission into the Wastelands with Hales. Every part of him was on edge, preparing for danger. It felt good.

Okafor pointed toward the back of the room. "Yaeko, you take the rooftops. Stay hidden, and keep your eyes on the sky for drones."

"Sure, whatever," said Yaeko, looking at her nails. She was the only one of the Healhome kids who didn't seem excited. But then she never seemed excited about anything.

"Now, does everyone understand?" said Okafor.

Kobi nodded.

The general raised his voice. "I need to hear it."

"Yes!" said Leon and Kobi. Yaeko muttered something. Rohan saluted and barked, "Yes, sir!" Kobi and the others laughed. Okafor's eyes narrowed. It seemed pretty straightforward to Kobi. Walk to the clinic, scope it out, call in the delivery. But he'd been in the slums just once before, when they first arrived at the Sol base. They were a maze—chaotic and busy, full of noise. But it would be a walk in the park compared to traveling through the Wastelands. *Which I might be doing soon, if this goes well.* The thought made Kobi's adrenaline surge even higher.

"What about me?" asked Asha, an edge to her voice.

"You'll be in the van," Mischik told her. "We want you to keep track of the thoughts of the others. The team will have earbuds and mics to speak with each other. But you can report on their state of mind and what they're thinking. In a high-pressure situation, untrained operatives can forget to communicate accurately."

Kobi frowned, trying to read Mischik's impassive face. He wondered if there was another reason for using Asha to keep tabs on their thoughts. If one of them was thinking about running away, Asha would know and report it back to Mischik. Kobi—and Mischik—knew from experience that Asha would do what she thought was right, even if it meant turning on Kobi.

"We'll be monitoring you through ocular cameras as well," said Okafor. "You're not on your own out there." He threw a glance at Mischik as if to say, *Are you really sure about this?*

Kobi held his breath for a second, but Mischik turned away from the general and clapped his hands. "Okay, if there are no more questions, report to the mission Hub on A-Level for your apparel and equipment. And good luck." He looked at Kobi. "I know you won't let me down."

Kobi's heart beat faster as they prepared to leave the base. They were all dressed in slightly grubby civilian clothing to help them blend in, and a Sol agent had helped apply makeup and putty to their skin. Leon had mottled scarring across his cheeks, and they'd made Rohan's forehead protrude unnaturally. Fairly standard Waste-related side effects. Kobi had been given a hunchback. They left Yaeko as she was—with her camouflaging skin pigmentation she could stay out of sight.

The "ocular cameras" were like contact lenses. After the briefing, Spike had showed them how to fit the devices over their eyes. "We've been working on these for a while. We can see what you're seeing all the time. Don't need to be taken out or cleaned ever. You don't feel a thing. Neat, huh?" He lowered his voice. "Mischik wanted you guys to wear these permanently in the base, but we managed to persuade him that might be a little too creepy." The lens implants felt weird at first, but Kobi had soon gotten used to them. It was an odd feeling knowing others were looking wherever he was, almost claustrophobic.

As they headed along the corridor toward the exit, Kobi imagined Spike, Mischik, and the others gathered around a screen watching the feed from his ocular camera—right now, just the back of Leon's head. They reached a sturdy metal door, which Kobi guessed led to the outside.

This is it, Kobi thought. There was a fingerprint pad on one side and a large metal wheel on the door itself.

"Okay, team," said Okafor. "You have your instructions. And remember, if you run into *any* problems, call us in."

He pulled his chair up alongside the fingerprint pad, touched it, and nodded to Leon, who spun the wheel to open the thick steel door. A set of metal steps led up the other side, where a faint light seeped around the edges of a closed hatch.

Kobi's heart raced. Everything seemed to slow down around him. It was the odd clearheadedness he got in dangerous situations.

It was time to go.

Kobi went first and pushed the hatch open at the top. It let out inside what looked like an old school bus, the windows covered by thin curtains. As the others emerged behind him, he walked slowly to the front and stepped through the open door into a garage. Mechanics were working on several vehicles nearby, and a couple nodded or even winked when they caught sight of Kobi. They were all Sol people, he knew. The garage was a front for the access point—though it was a working business too. A battered van was jacked up at one side, with a mechanic's legs sticking out from beneath. She slid out, nodded to Asha, and indicated the rear doors.

Asha turned to Kobi. "Good luck," she said. "I know you can do this." After a second, she gave him a hug. Kobi, taken a little by surprise, patted her on the back.

"Thanks," he said uncertainly.

"Whoa. Easy, guys," Leon said with a smile.

Kobi shook his head at him, and Rohan grabbed them both in a hug. "Don't leave me out!"

Yaeko just rolled her eyes.

"Let's do this," said Kobi.

They emerged from the smell of engine oil and fuel into open air—a steep street lined with hardware shops, electrical supply stores, tool rental places, and businesses collecting and selling scrap metal. Someone was sharpening a blade on a whetstone, filling the air with a high-pitched buzz. Random machine parts were scattered among the stalls—generators, spools of cable, pumps, engines, computer servers sprouting wires. No one paid any attention to Kobi and the others. Another kid passed on a hover scooter. Kobi instinctively ducked, and he caught Leon scoffing at him. Kobi noticed, as the boy whizzed over the corrugated iron rooftops, that his back was bent over and the hair was missing from part of his head. He felt thankful for his immunity to Waste.

A prickling sensation spread over his scalp. *Hi, Asha*, Kobi thought.

They hurried forward in loose formation, Kobi's eyes darting around. The voice of Jonathan Hales drifted across his mind.

"Everything is important. See everything at once, but don't get distracted."

"No flesh-eating ivy here. Don't worry," he muttered.

"What was that, Caveman?" Leon whispered into his mic.

"Nothing."

Nearly all the people in the slums had been deformed by some kind of Waste side effect. He tried to control his shock, but Kobi couldn't help staring. Apparently, that kid on the hover bike had it good. Almost every face was scarred, some seeming partially paralyzed. Many people had missing or misshapen limbs.

Kobi clenched his fists. The Waste in the slums, Spike had said, was ten times as concentrated as in the central, wealthy districts. CLAWS didn't care.

"What's up?" said Leon in his earpiece. Kobi glanced back and saw him and Rohan pretending to inspect a storefront selling battered holo-TVs.

"Nothing," Kobi said, pushing on, and concentrating on navigating. He'd memorized the route to the clinic. "Just . . . all these people—I didn't realize how bad it was."

"Yeah," said Leon in a hushed voice.

Kobi took a turn through a narrow alley full of faded laundry hanging on lines from ramshackle two-story homes. He looked around. "Where's Yaeko?"

"Above you, two o'clock," came the girl's voice. "Can we move a little faster, please?"

Kobi looked up and saw her lying low against a corrugated roof, her skin blending in to the gray metal and red rust. She was wearing a plain dull gray tunic and shorts to help with the camouflage.

He set off up the street in a casual walk. Okafor had told them CLAWS had human spies as well as drones. Any unusual behavior was liable to draw attention. Again he felt the pins and needles across his head as Asha tracked his emotions. He tried to feel a sense of confidence and focus to reassure her.

At the top of the street, the shop stalls gave way to more housing, a mishmash of construction plastic and crumbling concrete. The smells of spices and frying oil filled the air. Kobi noticed no wildlife—no insects or stray cats or dogs. Pets were exterminated by CLAWS drones in case they'd mutated from Waste contamination. Insects were kept from the city by great burning chemical fires that occasionally blew over from the outskirts, and Spike had said there were ultrasonic deterrents too, out of range of human hearing.

A woman hurried past carrying two buckets of water across her shoulders. Others had small wheelbarrow carts, some motorized, loaded with everything from loaves of bread to pieces of furniture. At the intersection between two streets, Kobi looked to the side and paused. In the far distance, the skyscrapers of New Seattle rose like gleaming needles in the sky. Flying vehicles swarmed between them like insects, and a monorail snaked several hundred feet above the streets, bisecting some buildings like a tunneling caterpillar.

"All clear to the west," said Yaeko. Kobi had no idea where she was, but he trusted her judgment. Rohan and Leon were sticking to their orders, following at about ten paces back. But occasionally he overheard their whispers to each other over the mic. "Man, I feel sorry for that dude. He's got three eyes." Leon's voice.

"Hey, I wouldn't mind another one." Rohan.

"That would be a scary image. Think them being yellow is freaky enough."

Keeping the modern city straight ahead, Kobi made his way along the street, ducking to the side as a motorbike zipped past, cutting through a puddle of filthy water. After another turn, they came to a high point, affording a view of much of the slum below. It was like a shanty mountain, with thousands of dwellings tightly packed together. A city in itself—the forgotten people who couldn't afford to live in the sterility of New Seattle in fortieth-floor apartments. Kobi shook his head. He knew what it was like to struggle for food every day, but here it felt so needless.

Between the slums and the new city extended a vast plain filled with industrial buildings. New Seattle had been constructed less than a year after the Waste disaster, a hundred miles east of the original city. A place to house survivors. A symbol of hope. Kobi remembered Mischik telling him that most of it belonged to CLAWS and their various business interests, whether in pharmaceuticals, food production, or technology. The biggest brand in the world.

Across the sky over the central district, Kobi could make out the floating dark silhouettes of drones, like a plague. Most of them, he knew, were CLAWS drones scanning for Waste infection. It seemed they didn't bother scanning the slums.

"Got any change?" came a voice from Kobi's left. A face peered out from a pile of ragged blankets. It was a young woman, both eyes pale and blind, and as she reached out, Kobi saw her hand had only three fingers. He mumbled he was sorry, and wandered on.

"Hey, you missed a left turn," said Rohan in his ear. "Stay sharp."

Kobi backtracked and took the alleyway. It too was crowded with people, many of them carrying groceries in huge bags slung over their shoulders or bundled across their backs. Acrid smoke drifted from a yard where it looked like a man was boiling tar. Kobi tried to keep focused. They met a crowded crossroads, and Kobi looked back for his escorts but couldn't see them. His heart sped up.

"You still with me, guys?"

"They're about twenty yards back," said Yaeko, watching from on high.

As Kobi turned again, his way was blocked by a sharply dressed woman with gray hair chopped into an immaculate bob, and cold, penetrating eyes in a small and sharp-featured face—a face Kobi recognized immediately with a stab of horror in his gut.

"Melanie Garcia," hissed Kobi into his radio. All his survival instincts had gone out the window. He felt paralyzed, unable to move, as helpless as when he'd been strapped to the operating table at Healhome and Melanie had given the order to cut him open—alive. Seeing her face brought that terror flooding back. The ruthless CEO of CLAWS took a step over to Kobi. "We're looking for terrorists," she said. "Perhaps *you* can help us."

Kobi, still moving backward, banged into a cart of fruit.

"Hey, watch out!" said the man pushing it.

Melanie advanced, thin lips stretching out in smile. "We can make it worth your while," she said. She reached into her pocket. Kobi expected a weapon, but the woman drew out a handful of hundred-dollar bills. "Think about it—the reward could be yours. . . ." She threw the bills in the air, and they fluttered down, then pixelated and vanished.

"I . . . I don't understand," Kobi stammered.

Melanie smiled, then a phone number flashed across her face. "Call the CLAWS tip line now," she said. "Call us *today*!" And then the entire image flickered and shrank in on itself to reveal a small drone, only as big as Kobi's fist. It shot up in the air.

"It's just a holo-ad," said the man with the cart. "Chill out, buddy."

Kobi's heart began to slow again. "*Stay in control always. Never get flustered, Kobi*," said Hales's voice. Kobi gathered himself before heading on, giving the all clear on his radio.

The street soon opened out into a patch of bare scrub, where a few shoeless kids were playing soccer.

"Think we could take them?" asked Leon, catching up with Kobi. Kobi sensed he wanted to reassure him that his backup was still close by.

"Team Sol take *anybody*?" answered Rohan, strolling up behind them. "Not a chance."

"I don't know," said Kobi. "We have a few advantages."

"You're almost at the clinic," interrupted Yaeko curtly. "Cross the square ahead."

Makeshift cafés had been set up around another open space, with an assortment of battered tables and chairs. People were chatting or laughing, enjoying themselves. A couple of cheap holo-screens played what looked like music videos or news feeds. But across the field, Kobi saw a long line of people—men, women, and children of all ages. The line snaked around blocks of buildings, twisting and turning down a slope into the distance. Kobi couldn't see its end, but just what he could see had to be hundreds of people on its own.

As Kobi got closer, he saw that many of the people looked desperately ill. Some were moaning in pain or had mutations far more pronounced than anything Kobi had seen making his way here. He peered toward the front and saw a green cross painted over a doorway.

"I guess that's the clinic," he said. "Look out for any sign of CLAWS, everyone."

He moved past the line, avoiding the baleful looks of the waiting patients.

Now he understood why Mischik had let them come here. He must have wanted Kobi to see this. To witness the suffering with his own eyes.

With that realization came anger—and not just at CLAWS. Kobi had spent his whole life being manipulated—first by Hales, then briefly by Asha—even if her intentions were good and she was being lied to at the time—and then Melanie. Now it was Mischik. *He wanted me to know why Sol's work matters. Why my safety matters.* It was probably the only reason he had allowed Kobi to go on this mission, to renew Kobi's commitment to the cause, to keep him *focused*. Kobi scowled. *I'm nothing more than a resource to them*, he thought. *No—I'll prove them wrong.*

As they passed through the open doors of the clinic, an elderly man tried to stop them. "I've been waiting overnight! You kids can't jump ahead."

Leon and Rohan appeared as if from nowhere, but Kobi gave them a quick shake of his head. "Sir, we're just helping to deliver supplies. My—my mother works here." The man frowned at him, but his mouth stayed pursed.

Kobi stepped inside. That was no better: people were packed in front of the reception desk, some pleading, as a few harried doctors tried to keep them calm.

"Please, my son's too sick to leave the house. We need more drugs," a woman was saying.

The doctor checked his tablet. "We've already given you the full recommended dose this month," he said.

"But it's not enough. Please, he's really sick!" The mother looked around hurriedly. Kobi looked away so she wouldn't think he was watching her. "I need the . . . other stuff."

The doctor, mouth hidden behind a surgical mask, shook his head. "I'm sorry, ma'am. I don't know what you mean."

The woman lowered her voice. "Please . . . I know we're not supposed to say it, but I need it. Horizon. The . . . the CLAWS drugs aren't working anymore. He's getting sicker every day."

"Keep your voice down," said the doctor in a whisper. He cast his gaze around and took out a small scanning device that Kobi guessed was used to pick up drone signals. When it lit up green, he went on. "Let me see what we can do," he said. "Wait here, please."

"Thank you!" said the woman. "Thank you so much!"

"Hey, shouldn't we get on with the mission?" Leon murmured in Kobi's earpiece.

Kobi turned to where Leon hovered with Rohan just inside the doorway, occasionally peering out into the street. They had managed to blend in with the waiting crowd, although the old man was still grumbling in their direction. Kobi realized he'd been standing there watching for too long. Get in and out as quickly as they could: that was the mission.

Kobi glanced around and spotted an inner door that read: "PRIVATE. AUTHORIZED STAFF ONLY." He went to it, weaving through the crowd of patients, and was about to push it open when a hand caught his arm.

"Hey, where d'you think you're going?"

It was a woman in a lab coat and mask. She had a wild rush of thick red hair streaked with wiry gray. Her pale skin was unblemished from the Waste, but her eyes were ringed with redness.

Kobi made a useless gesture with one hand. "I—I mean, we . . . we're here to—"

"You need to get in line like everyone else," she said. "We'll get to you when we can."

"Password, Kobi," Rohan whispered.

"'We thrive in the sun's light,'" he said, remembering the secret phrase Okafor had told them.

The doctor's face changed, at first shocked, then considering. "'And we lament as the sun falls,'" she replied. "Are you alone?"

Kobi shook his head. "There are four of us."

With a quick glance toward the entrance, the doctor opened the internal door. "Follow me."

"I'll stay outside and keep watch," said Yaeko.

Rohan and Leon abandoned their posts at the door and followed Kobi and the doctor deeper into the clinic. Beyond the door was a storage room lined with racks and shelves. As soon as they were out of hearing range of the patients, the doctor pulled down her mask. "You're very young," she said.

"We know what we're doing," said Rohan.

"You're sure you weren't followed? CLAWS has increased their patrols in the slums."

"We're sure," Leon said. "We're not exactly normal kids."

The doctor raised an eyebrow. "You're the kids on the run from CLAWS?" she asked. "I heard a rumor that they conducted experiments on you. You have some kind of augmented abilities. Should have known you'd end up with Sol."

"At your service," said Leon proudly. "Don't worry. We know how to deal with CLAWS."

Rohan caught Kobi's eye, then puffed out his chest in imitation of Leon.

"Well, I'm glad you came," said the doctor, "because we're running low on Horizon. Demand is already high, and word is spreading. It works so much better than anything CLAWS has been handing out. Their drugs only suppress the Waste's effects—Sol's seem to wipe them out completely. Until the patient is recontaminated, anyway." She shook her head. "The Waste is spreading out here, but no one cares."

"The shipment is ready," said Kobi. "Just give the word and we can call it in."

Suddenly the door burst open, and a man stumbled into the room. He was clutching a sharpened piece of scrap metal in his fist, which he brandished at them. They all stepped back. "Give it to me!" he said. "I need Horizon!" He clearly did, Kobi thought with a sinking feeling. His face was covered in open sores, his lips were cracked, and his eyes were a sickly yellow.

Leon held out his hands defensively. "Stay back!"

The man lunged—but then he tripped. He fell to the ground, and Kobi saw his back was slick with sweat. The veins across his arms were bulging.

"We can help you," said the doctor, casting her eyes about. Kobi wondered if she was looking for medicine or a weapon.

The man began to crawl toward them, and they retreated farther. Kobi backed up against a shelving unit, keeping his eyes fixed on the desperate patient.

"Now," the man groaned. "I need it now. . . ."

Suddenly he leaped up in a burst of strength and charged toward the doctor. Rohan moved quickest, flinging himself in the way, but the man dodged him and fell into Kobi. Pain shot through Kobi's shoulder, and he shoved the man away harder than he intended, flinging him into a set of shelves, which went crashing to the ground.

"Whoa—easy!" Leon shouted.

"I'm sorry," mumbled Kobi. "I didn't mean to . . ." He caught a flash of red and looked down to find blood seeping into the front of his shirt. Then he saw the end of the makeshift blade protruding from his shoulder. "Oh."

Leon was staring in shock between the wound and the man moving weakly on the floor when another member of the staff hurried through the door. "Sorry, doctor. He pushed past . . ." His eyes widened. "God, what happened?"

Kobi reached for the metal shard.

"No! Don't touch that—" the redheaded doctor began, but Kobi slid the blade out of his flesh, clenching his teeth and groaning at the explosion of pain. The doctor moved quickly, pressing a roll of gauze to Kobi's bleeding shoulder. "Now the wound will bleed more. Come on, through here." She led them past the shelves to another door. "You take care of him," she said to the other staffer, and pointed to the infected patient still writhing on the floor.

Beyond the door was some sort of exam or treatment room, judging by the bed surrounded by old-fashioned hospital equipment. "Sit down. We'll need to get your shirt off," said the doctor.

Leon cleared his throat, entering with Kobi. "Um, doc—he'll be fine."

"Really, I'm okay," Kobi protested. He was thinking of the mission. What would Mischik say? This would only prove his point. "We should call in the delivery of Horizon."

The doctor was pulling on a pair of gloves. "Are you kidding?

It's you who needs the cleansers now. That man who attacked you was a Stage Four, maybe Five. There's a very high chance the Waste will be directly in your bloodstream."

"It doesn't affect me," said Kobi, but the doctor was already cutting into his shirt with a pair of scissors.

"Lie back." Kobi did as he was told, then the doctor used a sponge to clean the blood from his shoulder. She frowned. "That's odd. It looked much deeper than that. Right. Let me find a bandage." As she went to a cupboard in search of a sterile dressing, Rohan turned conspiratorially to Kobi.

"Should I tell her, or do you want to?"

"Tell me what?" asked the doctor. She came back to Kobi's side and then froze in astonishment. Kobi glanced at his shoulder and saw the wound had almost completely healed up. "That's . . . not possible," she said.

"Told you we weren't exactly normal," Rohan said, grinning.

"I don't understand," said the doctor. "You healed yourself?"

"I'm different," said Kobi.

"Okaaay," the doctor said, grabbing a syringe. "Well, let's give you a shot of Horizon anyway."

"I don't need it," said Kobi. "I could use a new shirt, though."

The doctor gave him a curious look. "You can heal Waste infection too."

"I'm sort of immune."

For a few seconds the doctor was speechless, then she said quietly, "So it's true." She put down the syringe. "I mean, we'd heard rumors. That one of the fugitives—the kids from the CLAWS experiments—was the source of the Horizon drugs. To be honest, I didn't believe it."

"Well, here he is," Leon said. "The Caveman."

"The Caveman?"

Kobi nodded. "I grew up in Old Seattle. Kinda wild out there." The doctor stared at him. "A scientist at CLAWS kidnapped me from CLAWS when I was a baby," he explained. "Thought we would be safer, and he could use the Waste environment to help create Horizon."

The doctor looked a little faint as she sat down. "If that's true—why not make yourself known to the world? You could give people hope that there's a way past this disease! Why aren't we giving over all our resources to creating more Horizon?"

Kobi met her gaze. "CLAWS."

The doctor paused and furrowed the thin, freckled skin of her brow. "Are you saying they wouldn't want knowledge of you to get out?"

"Well, they tried to kill me. . . . So, no. They've been suppressing the supply of Horizon, trying to destroy Sol. They block all our communications and call us terrorists."

The doctor had gone pale, and she ran her fingers through her hair. "I knew CLAWS had a lot of power. I could have guessed they'd want to hold on to it. But I thought essentially they were good. I didn't think . . ."

"Your contacts at Sol haven't told you much, have they?"

She shook her head. "I don't ask questions. I don't want to risk losing our supply of Horizon. The drugs were everything Sol had said they would be. But apparently I've been a fool about CLAWS. We're all so desperate for something powerful enough to keep us safe from the Waste. . . . I guess we never see what they truly are." She looked up at Kobi. "Tell Sol they can trust me. My name is Maria Cahill. But please, the way to stop this is to show the world. I have contacts at a few nonprofits, at medical journals . . ." But she trailed off as Kobi shook his head.

"Sol thinks it's too risky to draw that much attention," Rohan cut in. "CLAWS has spies everywhere—if they knew where Kobi was, they'd squish him like a bug."

"But this news might be what the people need," said the doctor. "They'd rise up—"

"And CLAWS would squish them too," said Rohan. "It's not worth it."

"How can you say that?" said the doctor. "There's nothing more important than fighting the Waste. You've seen how it is out here. They need you."

Kobi found it uncomfortable under the doctor's prolonged gaze. It was the same look the other scientists gave him at Sol's base. *Hope. That's what it is. That's what people see in me.*

The worst part of it was Kobi thought she might be right. Maybe he could make a difference and not just with his blood. He thought of the poor people waiting in the line. Waiting and longing for a cure that might never come, all because of CLAWS.

But if they did rebel, in great enough numbers, it might be enough to break the hold CLAWS had over New Seattle.

"I would be happy to do it," said Kobi truthfully. "But I have to trust Sol. They know CLAWS better than anyone." As he spoke he found himself believing in Mischik's plan again, feeling proud that he was part of the resistance.

"Word *will* spread about Horizon," said Rohan. A spark lit his eyes. "Revolutions start underground."

"We need the all clear to deliver the Horizon," said Kobi, realizing they were lingering too long.

The doctor took Kobi's hand. "Tell Sol whatever they need, I'm in. I want to help. And thanks for coming here. One day, people will know your name." She let his hand go. "You can call in the delivery. Around back—as usual."

Kobi gave the code phrase over the radio. "'Dawn breaks.'"

As the other two boys turned to leave, the doctor touched Kobi's arm, and he hesitated. "Please think about what I said," she whispered. "We do what we can here, but we're fighting a forest fire with buckets of water. You could put the whole thing out."

Kobi nodded to her, but he felt the weight of responsibility like an anchor in his stomach. He hurried out into the clinic's lobby, Rohan and Leon on either side of him. It was still chaos in the waiting room. Kobi and the others filed out past the line and into the square.

The first thing he noticed was Yaeko, who was standing at the front of a ring of people all surrounding a girl in colorful clothes, with olive skin and dark straight hair. *What is Yaeko doing? Who is that?* He quickened his steps toward her—and then realized that the other girl, the one holding everyone's attention, was Niki. The Healhome girl looked a little taller and her hair was longer, and the jumpsuit she wore at Healhome had been replaced with an outfit that looked expensive and bright.

Kobi quickly ducked under a scrap metal–stall awning. What was *she* doing here?

"It's okay," said Leon. "It's just another ad drone." But his voice was uneasy. "Yaeko shouldn't have come down here into the open though."

As Kobi watched, Yaeko raised a hand and passed it through Niki's chest. Around her, people were watching her like she was crazy.

"No!" exclaimed Rohan. "What's she thinking?"

Rohan darted off in her direction, Kobi and Leon on his heels. Yaeko was completely transfixed; she didn't look at them even when they reached her side. The hologram was talking, not to anyone in particular but turning on the spot to address people around the street.

"I thought no one cared, but I was wrong. Melanie cared. She adopted me, a Waste-infected orphan. They thought I'd be dead within a year. So did I. But I was wrong. With Premium Regime I'm almost completely cured, and stronger than ever. Just one pill once a week, and it's enough to wipe ninety-nine percent of the Waste infection from my system." She held up a small blue pill and popped it

in her mouth. *"Easy as that! Get your Premium Regime today from your local health center. Thanks to CLAWS, I have a life to live. CLAWS: Healing the Past, for a Better Future."*

The image faded, and the drone floated upward.

"She looks so happy," Yaeko said, finally glancing at Rohan.

"That's because she's *brainwashed*," he hissed at her.

"Come on. It's not safe here," Kobi whispered in Yaeko's ear. "We need to go. Now."

Above them, the drone had stopped. It rotated in the air, pointing what looked like a lens toward them. Then it bobbed closer. Kobi couldn't shake the feeling it was performing some sort of scan.

"Uh-oh," said Leon. "I really don't like that."

The drone came closer still, its lens moving between their faces. Others in the crowd had started to pay attention. Suddenly, Rohan shot out a hand, grabbed the drone, and thrust it into a nearby trash can. After he slammed the lid on top of it they could hear the drone bouncing blindly around inside.

"Let's go!" Rohan said.

They made it less than five steps before people started to shout in alarm, and Kobi made out a whirring sound he knew all too well. And then he saw the first Snatcher.

It came from the south, low over the rooftops. The quarantine drone was the size of a car, kept aloft by thrusters under stabilizing wings. Its eight metal legs unfolded, their talons flexing, and the visual array of segmented eye-parts glittered. It was followed by a second, identical drone. They circled once above the square, emitting beeping sounds. The crowd scattered, and for a second Kobi and his friends were exposed.

They didn't wait for the Snatchers to descend. They ran for their lives.

4

THE SHADOWS OF THE Snatchers were closing in.

"Follow me!" Kobi said, veering off down a narrow alley. He heard a bang and looked back to see the Snatcher stuck at the entrance, trying to squeeze between the buildings with a screech of metal. It gave up and shot into the sky.

"We need to lose them," Leon huffed.

Kobi slowed his steps, darting into another passage that was no wider. He closed his eyes a moment and tried to still his panicked thoughts. The drones had all sorts of sensors—thermal, Waste detection. There was nowhere to hide. "We need extraction. Now!" he said into his radio.

Most people were heading indoors, slamming doors behind them. Kobi had learned that Snatchers were used in New Seattle too, to remove contaminated people trying to cross from the slums to the central district.

An elderly man collapsed in the road ahead, and several people just jumped over his body in an effort to flee. Kobi stooped to help the man up. "Don't let them take me!" the man said.

"Get to cover," Kobi said to him, pointing to a makeshift bar in a crumbling brick building, where people were huddling under tables.

Kobi spotted Rohan and Leon yards away, beckoning to him from a crossroads. "Quick, Kobi, hurry!" Rohan said over the radio.

He sprinted, legs powering him through the emptying street, until he reached their position. Yaeko was ahead in a wide lane across the intersection, leaping between the awnings of market stalls and the sides of buildings. She looked back at them. "What're you waiting for?" she called over the radio.

They hurried after her, keeping under cover, beneath the awnings of the stalls. "I think we might have lost them," Leon said.

The stall in front of them collapsed in a heap as a Snatcher thumped down, crushing the merchandise. People ran screaming. A hundred blinking red eyes whipped toward them, covering the rounded steel head of the giant insectoid drone. It let out a series of beeps and whirs, and a stinger-like tail rose from beneath its metal carapace. Kobi heard some sort of mechanism shift and lock into place. He could just make out a vial of yellow liquid being loaded into the barrel of the stinger.

Pfft!

Kobi braced himself, but in a flash Rohan's hand whipped out in front of his chest. He'd caught the dart around the shaft.

"They're firing poison darts now!" shouted Rohan, staring at the syringe in his hand. The yellowy liquid swirled within the glass casing. Snatchers could vary the concentration of toxin—either tranquilizing or killing organisms that had been contaminated by Waste. The chemical temporarily paralyzed mutated cells throughout the body, but in a big enough dose it could cause organ failure. When Kobi had last encountered the Snatchers, the toxin was delivered by an extendable stinger hidden beneath the drones' underbellies. Now the Snatchers were even deadlier.

"Looks like a lethal dose from the color," said Kobi, analyzing quickly. He stared around and in a second plotted a twisting route through the market stalls that would delay the Snatcher as much as possible while keeping himself and the others under cover. He pulled Rohan away, and he was about to shout for Leon, who he couldn't see, when he heard the whir of the Snatcher reloading. It scuttled after him. Kobi had just turned toward it when he heard a shout, and Leon appeared at the Snatcher's side. He was carrying an electric stun baton. Okafor had given one of the weapons to each of the kids except Kobi. Apparently it was part of the protocol. "I don't want you to worry about fighting," Mischik had said. "If there's danger you run. Run immediately. The others can stay and fight." Kobi wondered if Mischik was worried about arming Kobi in case he went looking for trouble—seeking revenge against CLAWS for everything they had done to him.

Now I'm just defenseless, he thought.

A crackle of electrical sparks leaped from the end of Leon's baton and connected with the Snatcher's hull. At once the eight legs spasmed, and the creature hit the ground belly first. Its eye-scanners flashed randomly, and then it juddered before lying still.

"Come on," Leon said. "It's only temporary." When the Snatcher's system had rebooted it would be back fighting again. *Maybe some guns would have been more effective*, thought Kobi with a hard grimace.

Yaeko's voice came through his earpiece. "Past the bread stall," she said. "There's a road heading down the hill to the extraction point."

Kobi saw it. The stall-holder was hiding under a table, peering up at the sky, where the other drone was hovering. The fallen Snatcher began to quiver. Its legs locked straight on one side, making it lean unevenly, then the others did the same.

Leon's right. We can't wait around.

Rohan and Leon flanked him as they ran toward the road. Kobi could only hope Yaeko was looking after herself. They heard shouts and the hum of thruster engines. The Snatcher was airborne again, drifting just off the ground. It locked on to them, advancing slowly, in no hurry.

And then Kobi saw why. The street was a dead end.

"We're trapped," said Rohan. His large yellow eyes dazzled with fear.

"No," said Yaeko. Kobi realized he could hear her and not just in his earpiece. He glanced up and saw her clinging to the side of the wall above them. "There's a window to your left."

Kobi spotted the window and shattered the glass with the heel of his boot. "We can lose the Snatcher in here," he said. Leon cleared the shards of glass with his baton, then jumped inside, followed by the others. Kobi came last. He found himself in a humid room lit with dingy strip lighting. It was a laundromat, with clothes hanging on lines and washing machines all around whirring. A few people holding clothes were staring at Kobi and the other kids.

Kobi heard a whirring from the other side of the broken window. "Snatcher cut me off," said Yaeko. "I'll meet you on the other side of the building."

There were a slam and a groaning of metal as the first Snatcher tried to ram its large body through the small window. "See ya!" Leon called to it, waving his electric baton. Rohan had drawn one too.

"Everyone, hide!" shouted Leon to the people doing their laundry, though the order was pointless. They were already running, screaming, for a door at the far end of the laundromat. Slabs of brickwork broke off around the window as the Snatcher battled to get into the room.

Kobi shivered at the thud of Snatcher darts, and the smashing of broken washing machine glass surrounded him. "Keep low!" he said. They followed the fleeing crowd through a set of double doors into a small kitchen, then through a set of hanging plastic drapes into a storeroom lined with crates.

"It's still coming!" cried Rohan.

The double door burst inward. The Snatcher lowered its head to fit through, feet skittering on the tiled floor. Kobi and the others rushed out a fire escape into a small backstreet filled with trash cans, then slammed the barred door closed behind them. Yaeko was waiting for them.

"The extraction team will be here any minute," she said.

The Snatcher thumped into the other side of the door, shaking it in its frame. Then again. Kobi and Leon threw themselves against it. "We can't hold it off for long," Leon said. A third impact knocked them all backward. Kobi expected the Snatcher to erupt through, but nothing happened. For a few seconds they all watched the door, breathing hard.

"Is it gone?" asked Leon.

"I think so," Rohan said.

Kobi wasn't so sure. He'd never known a Snatcher to give up the chase. They were relentless.

The growl of engines sounded from the end of the street, and four dirt bikes skidded around the corner. *The extraction team!* The bikes slewed to a halt, and the lead rider pushed back her visor.

"Get on!" she said.

In one smooth movement, Yaeko leaped onto the back of one of the bikes, and Leon climbed up behind another driver. But Kobi hesitated. *"Use your surroundings, Kobi. Always look for opportunity."* As he listened to Hales's voice in his head, he ran over to the trash cans. Rohan followed him. "What's up, Caveman?"

"Shields," Kobi said simply. He took off the lids from the trash cans and passed one to Rohan, then he ran over to Yaeko and Leon.

"Hurry up!" said the fourth Sol agent, waiting on his bike.

"What are these for?" asked Leon.

Rohan moved like a blur, throwing his arm across Leon's body. Kobi saw a dart clatter into the metal lid.

"That!" said Kobi.

Kobi twisted his neck to see where the dart had come from. Both Snatchers were zooming over the rooftops toward them, at a height of about ten yards. Their tails arced over their backs, firing darts as they flew.

Pffft! Pffft! Pffft!

Kobi raised his trash can lid and felt the projectile hit. Rohan blocked another, and a third whistled into the chassis of Leon's bike. *Thanks, Hales*, Kobi thought. His heart thudded, but his vision was clear, and he prepared for another shot, holding up the lid.

"Can we go already?" yelled Yaeko.

Kobi felt the bike lurch and gripped his rider to stay in the saddle. They bounced over the uneven terrain, throwing up dust. People scampered out of the way ahead. Kobi kept his eyes fixed on the sky, watching the Snatchers in pursuit. They were edging lower and firing darts all the time. Kobi kept the shield raised, just in case, but the darts missed him. His bike shot ahead of Leon's, taking the lead, and they steered a tight angle down another street. The Snatchers rounded the corner in perfect formation, lifelessly calm and all the deadlier for it.

"Leon, use that shocker!" Kobi shouted.

"They're too far up!" he called back.

One of the Snatchers broke away, perpendicular to their path, and vanished out of sight.

"It's trying to cut us off," said Kobi.

When he caught sight of the giant drone again, it was already a block ahead, moving parallel on another street. The one in pursuit suddenly dipped until it was trailing them almost at ground level, legs tucked under its carapace. Its staring eyes seemed fixed on Kobi's bike. *It wants me.* He felt his muscles tense with latent power. *I'm ready for you.* With a burst of acceleration it shot toward him.

With no other weapon, Kobi hurled the trash can lid. It smashed into one of the Snatcher's eyes. The drone dipped, one flank catching the ground and throwing up sparks. It flipped over, crashing through the front of a building. The Snatcher exploded, the heat making Kobi close his eyes, and he felt the sting of debris cutting his face.

"Don't ever drop your guard . . . ," Kobi scolded himself.

"Until you're sure the threat has passed." Hales's voice finished it for him in his mind.

Kobi braced himself just in time as he turned back, and the bike suddenly skidded. His knee almost grazed the road. His senses felt overloaded, but the driver managed to stop and keep the bike upright.

"Not good," said Rohan from his bike, which stopped at Kobi's side.

The second Snatcher squatted ahead of them. Its stinger flexed, and before it could even aim, Leon was running right at it, his trash can lid held in front of his head, and roaring a battle cry. Darts cut through the air, clattering off the shield as he charged into the Snatcher's head. A crash of splintered metal, and the drone's legs buckled.

"He got it!" Rohan said, but even as he spoke, the Snatcher reared up, flinging Leon onto the ground. Rohan started to run to his friend's aid as Leon tried to scramble away, and the mangled Snatcher loomed over him, feet stabbing into the dusty ground.

But Kobi held Rohan back, then took his shield. He hurled the lid, and it completely smashed away a foreleg, tearing through the metal. Still the Snatcher advanced on Leon, beeping maniacally. Dread surged through Kobi, and he knew it was too late to help their friend.

He sprang forward desperately, covering ten yards in two strides, but he knew it wouldn't be enough. He wouldn't get there in time. Leon crawled back, screaming. "No!" shouted Kobi. A strange shimmer spread like a heat haze over the wall beside the drone.

Yaeko appeared. She had an electric baton in her hand and

pointed it at the Snatcher's neck. "You've really got to take a hint," she said to the drone. The metal creature spasmed, its legs curling beneath it, then lurched sideways into rusted scaffolding attached to a two-story brick warehouse. The whole building rippled.

Yaeko jumped back as a mound of bricks and metal poles crashed down over the Snatcher's body. Kobi was already there pulling Leon aside. The mound of broken building moved faintly as the Snatcher struggled beneath it.

One of the motorbike riders pulled up his visor and said in a deep, rumbling voice, "Do these things not die?"

"Oh, they die," said Kobi. He picked up one of the scaffolding poles and chucked it to Leon. Leon grinned. The Snatcher writhed to the surface of the debris. Leon gritted his teeth as he put all his weight into the blow, stabbing the pole deep into the Snatcher's cluster of eyes, back into its main circuits. It sagged to the ground, strange chittering sounds coming from its insides. Slowly, the light in its eyes dimmed.

"What happened to the other one?" asked Rohan.

"I took care of it," Kobi said. But looking back, he saw the other Snatcher clambering toward them like a wounded animal still determined to fight.

"Okay," he said, "I take that back."

The wailing beeping and whir of its movements caused an instinctive shiver of horror to ratchet through Kobi's body. Sounds he'd dreaded since he could remember, sounds that said, *"Run. Hide. Pray."* Kobi felt sudden rage, even though he knew the Snatcher was just a mindless machine. He remembered how terrified he'd been of Snatchers back in the Wastelands—the nightmares that had woken him screaming in his bed at Bill Gates High. Why couldn't they just leave him alone? He climbed down from the bike and approached the lumbering contraption.

Was CLAWS watching? Maybe even Melanie Garcia herself? Kobi stared into the device. "One day, I'll find you, Melanie. One day you will pay."

"What are you doing?" said one of the riders. "Stay away from that thing. It's still dangero—" A Snatcher leg lashed out weakly. Kobi caught it in his hands, watching the hydraulic claw open and close as if still trying to grab him. With a brutal twist he wrenched the leg from its housing, then swung it with all his strength at the creature's head. The first strike smashed the eye. He drew back, fueled by anger, and struck again, crushing the metal inward. Fizzing sparks showered out. Kobi swung a third time, and it was enough to make the Snatcher fall onto its side, the last four legs trembling as its systems shut down.

"Whoa," said Leon. "Feel better now?"

"A little," said Kobi, looking at the defeated Snatcher.

"They'll send more," said the Sol motorbike driver with the deep voice—clearly the leader. "We have to go."

Kobi, Leon, and Yaeko climbed back onto their bikes, and the riders took off again at breakneck speed.

"Take the alleys," said Kobi. "We'll be shielded from their

visual sensors." Kobi clung on as the sides of the alleys zipped by—it seemed impossible that they could move so fast through this maze of ramshackle buildings. Kobi noticed that a screen on the bike seemed to map the roads ahead in 3D. Writing on the screen read, "Auto-Drive."

From the angle of the sun and the brief glimpses of the central district Kobi saw through gaps in the slum buildings, he knew they were heading back toward the garage where they'd exited the Sol base. After a couple of turns they entered a street almost completely sheltered under awnings. Sol must have put them up to cover the street from surveillance from above.

The bikes slowed, their engines a soft rumble, as they turned up a slight incline and into the workshop beneath a sign: "Jack's Garage." Kobi's driver cut the engine and kicked down the kickstand. Kobi leaped off. His whole body shook with adrenaline, and for the first time in a long while he felt alive. But he knew they'd been lucky. He wasn't looking forward to seeing Mischik.

The surveillance van was already parked in the garage. Asha jumped from the back, looking flustered. Spike clambered down after, grinning as he chewed a piece of gum.

"Are you guys okay?" Asha said. She came to Kobi first, looking him over for wounds. "We were watching everything through the ocular lenses."

"Awesome job, big guy!" said Spike to Kobi. "Man, that Snatcher fight was next-level. Hey, better switch off those lenses now." He tapped something on his smart watch, then said, "Deactivate ocular cameras." He winked at Kobi. "Don't want Mischik watching while you're in the john."

Kobi's rider dismounted and pulled off her helmet. She was a tall Asian woman, sweat plastering her hair to her scalp. "I can't believe we made it," she said with a smile at Kobi. "Thanks to you kids. What you did back there to those Snatchers . . . I've never seen anything like it."

"Pah, that was nothing," said Leon. His rider was the tall one with the deep voice: a bearded man with a scar over one eyebrow. "We need to report to Mischik. The fallout of this thing is going to be huge."

"Tell me about it," said Spike.

A medic emerged from the school bus that hid the secret entrance to the tunnels, and he began to check over the other kids.

"We're fine," said Yaeko abruptly. Kobi wondered if she felt guilty for alerting the Snatchers with her behavior toward the holo-commercial of Niki. Kobi could see that patches of skin around her face and neck were blending in with the metallic sheen of the garage, like she wanted to disappear. Kobi wanted to tell her that the holo-ads had confused him too, and if she hadn't been on the rooftops leading them, they never would have escaped the Snatchers. She'd made up for her mistake. But before he could approach, Leon was slapping him on the back.

"Asha, you should have seen Kobi. He beat a Snatcher to death with its own leg!"

Asha didn't look impressed. "Mischik wants us back in the base," she said, heading toward the school bus. "He's not happy."

Kobi swallowed. He wasn't looking forward to the debrief.

They'd begun to walk toward the bus when he heard someone fall behind him. Rohan was on his hands and knees, like he'd tripped. Leon rolled his eyes and sighed dramatically. "Rohan, we survive a Snatcher attack and you can't handle walking in a straight line?" But then he paused, eyes fixing on one spot before his face screwed up and he cried out, "Rohan!"

Then Kobi saw the dart protruding from the back of Rohan's calf. His pants were stained with blood.

"You've been hit!" said Leon. "We need to get him to medical—quickly!" In a second he was by his friend's side, crouching and levering his shoulder under Rohan's ribs before easing him up, carrying him like a child. "You're going to be okay, buddy."

Kobi spoke urgently to Rohan. "Stay with us, Rohan. You're going to be okay." But the words sounded thin. Rohan's arms dangled, and his eyes were closed. "Rohan, you have to stay awake!"

Asha had already dashed through the bus, and she threw open the hatch to the Sol tunnels, letting Leon carry Rohan through. Yaeko watched on silently. She had shifted her skin pigment to a sunflower yellow, blending almost completely into the school bus behind her.

"I didn't mean to," she whispered. "I didn't. . . ."

Kobi's gaze paused on her for a moment. Then he turned and followed the others back into the base.

* * *

"I never should have let you go."

Mischik had said the same thing, in slightly different ways, three or four times already as he paced up and down outside the corridor of the base's medical wing. Leon was hunched on the ground, his head bowed. Yaeko had appeared a little while after the others, watching silently. Kobi and Asha stared through the pane of glass set into the wall, where they could see Rohan lying silently on a bed, a mask over his mouth, monitors fastened to his bare chest, and with a drip in his arm. He hadn't moved or opened his eyes.

"What was I thinking?" said Mischik. "Okafor was right. No, *I* was right! I shouldn't have let you talk me into this." Kobi felt a jolt of hurt at the thought that Mischik was blaming *him* for Rohan's condition. But he let it go. This wasn't the time to argue about whose fault it was.

"Is he going to be okay?" Asha asked, chewing the inside of her cheek. Her dark eyes were watery.

Mischik took a deep breath, apparently cooling himself off. "The doctors are working as fast as they can. From what Kobi's told us, we need to neutralize it soon, or his vital organs could begin to shut down."

Kobi gave a small nod. Hales had analyzed the Snatcher toxin from the damaged CLAWS drone they had scavenged and then disassembled in the workshop at Bill Gates High.

"We've stabilized him," continued Mischik. "But he's still

critical. We've administered a high dose of the Horizon Waste cleansers in hopes that might counteract the toxin. Kobi's blood can neutralize all poisonous chemicals quickly, not just Waste."

Kobi nodded again, but he could read Mischik's face, and he knew what the man was thinking. CLAWS would have prepared the Snatchers to target Kobi, which meant the darts would have been designed to be so strong that they would overpower Kobi's antibodies.

Mischik's watch communicator buzzed, and he looked impatiently at the screen. "I have to go deal with the fallout from the clinic," he said. "The slums are flooding with drones, and we need to call back all our active operations. All of you, wait here. You need to be checked out by the docs too." He strode away.

"He'll be okay, right?" Kobi saw that Yaeko had approached tentatively. Her face was hard, but her voice was soft and her words shook. "With Kobi's blood, he'll pull through."

Leon looked up, eyes red. "If he does, it'll be no thanks to you."

"Hey, easy!" said Asha.

"Well, someone's gotta say it," said Leon. "What were you thinking, standing there gawking out in the open like that?"

"I thought it was really Niki!" said Yaeko.

Leon stood up and jabbed a finger toward her. "So what if it was? She's not on our side, remember? She chose CLAWS."

Yaeko stared back defiantly, her skin rippling red and orange. "It's not about sides," she snapped. "You're so simpleminded. Why don't you go and watch one of your dumb action movies?

Something you might understand." Even Kobi could tell Yaeko was lashing out as a defense mechanism, but she was only making things worse.

Kobi stepped between them. "Cool it. It's not helping."

"I understand orders!" Leon rose to his feet, ignoring Kobi. "I understand, 'Stay out of sight.' What's your excuse, lizard-breath?"

"That's enough!" said Kobi. "Rohan wouldn't want you squabbling like this, would he? Yaeko made a mistake, but none of us knew what it was going to be like out there. We didn't know the Snatchers would come so fast." Kobi had been taught to think rationally, to not let emotion cloud his judgment. Sometimes he wished everyone else had been too.

Leon blinked slowly. A vein at the side of his forehead was throbbing. "Rohan wouldn't be in there if it weren't for her," he said. "It's her fault. She's never been one of us. She wants to go back to CLAWS with her best friend, Niki. Maybe she did it on purpose."

Yaeko's jaw tightened. "Maybe I did!" she yelled.

Leon shoved past Kobi, going for Yaeko, but she leaped over him, her suction finger pads gripping the ceiling. She dropped to the floor in a fluid crouch, then strode away without looking back. Kobi grabbed Leon by the shoulders before he could go after her. Leon spun and shoved Kobi with a force that took the breath from his lungs. Before he knew it, Kobi was on the floor, skidding down the corridor.

"You should be happy!" Leon shouted at Kobi, tears breaking

from his eyes in a sudden stream. "This was your idea! We wouldn't have gone out there if you could keep still. You said it would be fine! You said . . ." He gave a last long look at Rohan, then hurried away.

Kobi got to his feet, rubbing at the bruising over his chest.

"Let him go," Asha said. "It's not worth fighting."

"I know."

A young Sol doctor, walking the other way, passed Leon in the corridor. She gave him a startled glance but kept moving. "Everything okay with you guys?" the doctor asked Kobi. He nodded. "Sorry, we still need to check you over. I guess we'll look at the others later."

Kobi shook his head. "Not now." He couldn't stop thinking about Leon's words. Maybe there was some truth to them. It had been Kobi's idea to go on the mission. And if that dart hadn't hit Rohan, it might have found its way to Kobi. He gazed at Rohan through the window: his face was pale and still as a medic bustled around him. It brought back painful memories of Healhome and seeing Jonathan Hales hooked up to monitors as his weak body tried and failed to battle the poison in his organs.

In a way, they both got hurt because of me. They were both just trying to keep me safe.

His scalp prickled, and he glared at Asha. She didn't need to be reading his emotions right now. "I just need some time by myself," he said, and before Asha or the doctor could protest, he hurried away.

He made his way slowly through the base. Sol operatives rushed through the corridors or were clustered in rooms speaking urgently. He heard snippets of conversation:

"PR nightmare."

"Police collaboration."

"Retract Horizon."

"Base could be compromised."

For once, no one paid him much attention. He caught a glimpse of Spike, but he was deep in conversation with other technicians in front of a bank of holo-computers.

He arrived at the dorms and saw that Leon's room was empty. Rohan's too, of course. Kobi collapsed onto his bed. The red light of the camera flickered from the ceiling. He fished under the bed and pulled out the map of Old Seattle. Asha had looked into his memories and helped him to recall Hales's exact notations, which they'd transcribed onto the new map: *L* for Labs, *M* for Medical Supplies, *F* for Food, as well as shading No-Go areas and marks for blocked roads and unstable buildings.

Kobi wondered what the school looked like now without their daily Waste protocols, sealing doors and windows to keep out contaminated spores. It was probably completely overrun with vegetation, the desks covered in moss, creepers across the ceiling, the gymnasium like a hothouse. It made him sad. Life had seemed so simple then, the days mapped out in a set routine of lessons, training, and following the protocols. Just Kobi and Hales. Son and so-called father.

It had been a lie, of course—all of it. Kobi folded the map away and stared at the bare concrete of his dorm wall. *This* was real. *This* was what he had to deal with now. After the disastrous trip outside, he wondered if Mischik would ever let him leave the base again. The dream of returning to the Wastelands and finding a permanent cure to the Waste was gone.

5

DINNER AT THE BASE'S cafeteria was normally a noisy affair, but the mood tonight was unsurprisingly somber. The mess hall had once fed the workers at the hydroelectric facility. It was all clean metal and long tables with benches, lit brightly by beaming lights hanging from the high ceiling. Leon sat alone, staring at his tray. Kobi thought about going over to talk, but he couldn't face another argument. Across from Kobi, Yaeko was pushing her food around with little interest.

From the sideways glances directed toward Kobi and the others, he guessed they were the main topic of conversation among the adults too. The holo-TV was playing a constantly updating feed of headlines.

It wasn't good news.

Apparently the clinic where they'd been just a few hours

before had been shut down while CLAWS investigated possible connections to Sol. Kobi could hardly watch as the begging crowds were dispersed and the doctors were led away by New Seattle's security forces. He saw Maria Cahill, the doctor who'd treated him earlier, among them, her hands cuffed as she was shoved into the back of a van. Dozens of Snatchers filled the sky above the slums. Teams of CLAWS anticontamination enforcers were patrolling on the ground.

Mischik, who normally ate with everyone else, was absent, shut away in an incident room with General Okafor, overseeing the damage control effort and organizing diversions to try to lure CLAWS away from the Sol base and also trying to arrange delivery of the Horizon drug to other clinics.

"Who'd want Horizon now?" asked a Sol tech at the neighboring table. "I mean, it's too risky, right? Might get a Snatcher coming through the roof and a CLAWS interrogation team breathing down your neck."

Kobi tried not to despair, but now the TV was showing a clip of the mayor of New Seattle. He was urging everyone to stick to CLAWS-only treatments and was even offering rewards to anyone in the slums who could provide information about the "terrorists."

"He's in CLAWS's pocket too," Asha said, sliding into a seat beside him.

"Do you think they'll find us?" asked Kobi.

"I don't know," she said.

“Don’t worry about that,” said one of the Sol agents at the next table. He was wearing a security uniform. “We’ve got fail-safes. If one of the entrances is compromised, we can flood the tunnels to provide a barrier.”

“Oh, good,” Asha said. “That sounds completely safe.” She lowered her voice so only Kobi and Yaeko could hear her. “I’ve sensed Fionn. He’s close. But I can tell he’s still trying to block me,” she said. “Why would he do that?”

“I have no idea,” said Kobi. “Where do you think he is?”

“Below us, somewhere,” said Asha. “He’s close though.”

Kobi paused. Mischik had been very clear when they first arrived that certain areas were out of bounds, and those included any of the floors beneath F-Level, where their dorms, the game room, and the cafeteria were situated. From the serious look on Asha’s face, he knew she remembered that too.

“Let’s find him,” he said. “We need to check that he’s okay. And he’ll want to know about Rohan.”

Yaeko agreed to cover for them. With the base on high alert and personnel mostly occupying the operations rooms or out in the field, the lower sections were uninhabited. Asha and Kobi made their way past the game room, glancing around to check that they weren’t followed, reaching a set of steel stairs. Kobi knew there were cameras all around the base, but he hoped no one would be bothering to monitor them too much with everything that was going on. Nevertheless, he tried to keep to blind spots where he could.

On the floor directly below were the generators that powered the base, still driven by underground water currents siphoned from the dam. Kobi held up his hand for the others to halt while he sensed for the presence of any Sol staff.

"Clear," he whispered back.

The air smelled slightly rancid, like something had died down there, and sure enough, they found the remains of a bird rotting on the ground. Kobi let his night vision adjust. Asha closed her eyes every so often. "This way," she said, and led Kobi along a walkway to what seemed to be some sort of storage area stacked with crates.

He saw a manhole cover in the ground, slightly ajar.

"This must be the manhole Yaeko mentioned," he said. "Maybe we should fetch Mischik."

"No," said Asha fiercely. "He's got bigger things to deal with tonight, and he'll just be angry. I don't want to get Fionn into trouble."

"Fionn might be in trouble already," said Kobi. "What if he's hurt himself?"

Asha shook her head. "That's not it," she said. "I sense . . . he just doesn't want to be found. If Mischik and a bunch of Sol agents come looking, he'll run. I know it."

Kobi crouched, gripped the thick metal of the cover, and scraped it aside. A ladder led into darkness. Mischik had told them in the early briefing that some of the ground under the base was unstable, prone to shifting or flash floods.

He went first, climbing down the rusty ladder and dropping

into a tunnel where the air was cooler. He could hear dripping somewhere, and there were discolored patches on the bare concrete walls. No doubt the tunnel had once carried water, though it must have dried up long ago. Asha landed beside him. He couldn't imagine why Fionn would ever want to come to this place.

"Which way?" Kobi asked. His eyes were fully adjusted now, casting the labyrinth of tunnels in monotones.

"I can't see well," said Asha. "Let me try something. Come closer." Kobi felt her hand curl around his temple, a soft cool touch. Then he felt the familiar sensation as she read his mind. He thought he could almost feel the tingling spread down to the back of his eye sockets.

"You're not . . . ?"

"Seeing through your eyes?" He stared at her grinning face. Her eyes looked a little unfocused. "You bet. I've done it with Fionn before but never anyone else. I'm not going to pretend this isn't weird. Hey, you could have told me I had flapjack on my cheek."

Kobi laughed. "What's it like seeing what I'm seeing? Isn't it confusing?"

"It's like . . . You know when you squint your eyes and you see two images at once? That, except they are not replicas but totally different."

"I'm getting travel sickness just thinking about it."

She grinned. "Just don't, you know, look around too fast."

"I'll try. I thought those ocular cameras were bad enough." Kobi blinked, remembering that his lenses still hadn't been removed. You forgot they were there after a while. Asha touched her temple and pointed off behind him. "I think I can sense Fionn through there."

They walked in single file, Kobi up front. He couldn't quite believe that Asha was looking out through his eyes. At the moment though, there wasn't much to make out. The architecture was almost featureless. Tunnels, running at an almost imperceptible slant, branched off at right angles every few yards, with the occasional flood grate in the wall. Some passages were wider and taller than others, and they passed the odd side-channel that would have been too small to enter, even on hands and knees. Kobi wondered how far the tunnels reached—maybe all the way under New Seattle. Yet despite the air of stillness and the solitary, muffled sounds of his and Asha's breathing, he sensed they weren't alone.

Ahead, a shape moved past a junction, accompanied by a flash of light—a flashlight, perhaps.

"There!" Kobi said, speeding up. Asha's footsteps shuffled after him.

"Wait!" she whispered urgently.

Kobi reached the intersection just in time to see the figure round a corner into a tighter shaft. On the ground was a packet of cookies, like the ones distributed from the Sol cafeteria. "Fionn!" He moved off, crouching down to enter the tunnel.

"Slow down!" called Asha, her voice echoing from several directions at once.

But Kobi didn't stop. In a hunt, you couldn't lose sight of the target. "I'll come back." He tripped and almost sprawled on his face, but he caught himself against the walls. The ground ahead ramped steeply down, with a channel cut into the floor. He braced himself, hands on the ceiling, and descended. At the bottom, the tunnel widened into a much larger concrete basin almost like a long, shallow swimming pool emptied of water. There were two semicircular openings at the end. The walls were cracked in places, with pieces of crumbling masonry scattered over the ground. He could hear movement close by. It had to be Fionn. Kobi moved back to fetch Asha.

"He's really close," she said.

Asha glanced back the way they'd come. "We've already taken a few turns," she said. "What if we get lost down here?"

Kobi shook his head. "Hales made me practice mental mapping all the time. I can find my way back."

"Are you sure?"

Kobi had to admit he wasn't: this place was a total maze with no sun or Horizon to use as a guide. All of it looked the same, just concrete and metal. It was amazing Fionn could find his way around. *"Orientation is everything. Use markers where you can—things you will remember or won't miss."* The voice of Hales drifted to him as if whispering through the tunnel, and Kobi heard his younger self reply.

"But, Dad, how do you mark anything in the Wastelands? It's always . . . growing. Changing."

"It's about choosing the right landmarks."

Kobi looked around at the tunnels. *If there aren't landmarks*, he thought, *I'll have to make them.*

"Ever read Hansel and Gretel?" he said to Asha.

"You know we didn't have many books at Healhome."

"Hales used to tell me loads of stories, beginning with old fairy tales," said Kobi. "Hansel and Gretel were a brother and sister, and their parents wanted to get rid of them."

"Sounds like a nice bedtime story," Asha said dryly.

Kobi couldn't resist a smile. "Yeah, fairy tales are often pretty dark. So their parents led them into the middle of the forest, then abandoned them. But Hansel overheard the plan, so he left bread-crumbs behind them, to mark the path home."

Asha frowned. "You don't actually want to use food as a trail, do you? Because that's kinda dumb . . ."

Kobi paced slowly down the tunnel until he found a rusted piece of disused pipe hanging from the wall. He reached out and tore the pipe away, twisting it until it snapped free, leaving a jagged point. Using the point, he scraped an arrow into the tunnel wall toward the exit.

"I like your thinking," said Asha.

They set off toward the semicircular openings, and every twenty steps or so Kobi scratched an arrow into the tunnel wall. He didn't tell Asha the whole story—not the parts about birds eating Hansel's crumbs or their getting kidnapped by a cannibal witch. *It's the principle that counts. . . .*

They entered another tunnel, barely tall enough to walk through in a crouch and heading down at a steeper angle. There were a few odd gouge marks in the walls, and Kobi kicked at more food wrappers. "He definitely came this way," Kobi said, scraping the rusted edge of the pipe along the ceiling in an arrow.

Asha pointed at a tunnel to the right. The ceiling had collapsed, leaving a pile of rubble, but it had been partially cleared. Kobi's stomach squirmed. If it was unstable down here, they could all be in danger. *So it's even more important that we get Fionn out.*

They passed the heap of fallen stones and pressed on.

"I can feel him," said Asha. She suddenly raised her voice and called Fionn's name, but all her cry did was drift in the darkness.

Kobi was breathing hard, and only when they stopped at the next intersection did he realize he could hear the flow of water. "We have to be out from under the base now," he said. "Maybe even close to the city."

Asha suddenly gripped her head as if in pain.

"What's the matter?" asked Kobi.

She blinked, her eyes watering. "I don't know. I thought I could just sense Fionn, but it's bigger than that. Much bigger."

His heart gave a single tangible thud like a strike to a base drum. A chittering sound came from the openings ahead. At first Kobi thought it sounded like a disrupted comms signal, but as it grew louder he realized it was some sort of animal, or animals.

"I think we should go back up," said Asha, her face turning to Kobi in the dark. Even in the dimness he could make out the panic in her oval eyes.

He nodded and turned around, only to be blinded by light. Kobi raised a hand, staggering backward. The light dimmed a fraction, and he realized it was a flashlight, now pointing at an angle toward the ground. The figure who held it was just a silhouette, but as Kobi's eyes recovered, he recognized him.

"Fionn?" Asha gasped.

The younger boy's hair was wild, and there were black smudges across his cheeks and around his eyes. His clothes were torn. He'd grown taller over the six months since they'd left Healhome, but now he seemed to stand taller still, even though it had been only a week since Kobi last saw him. A single tooth almost as long as his finger hung on a leather thong around his neck. It had once belonged to the mutated wolf he'd befriended in the Wastelands: the creature had fallen in a desperate fight with Snatchers during the escape from Healhome.

"*It's me*," said Fionn, sending his thought telepathically to Asha and Kobi.

The sounds from the shafts behind Kobi and Asha were getting louder by the moment. In his mind, Kobi felt Fionn's thoughts—dark and hostile, projected using his telepathy. *"You shouldn't be here."*

“Fionn,” said Asha nervously. “What’s that sound?”

Fionn shifted the flashlight again, directing it past them. Wriggling shadows painted the walls of the shaft. Shapes scurried in a mass of claws, squirming tails, and yellow, Waste-infected eyes.

Rats!

6

THE CREATURES CAME IN a wave, spilling over each other in their hunger to get to Kobi and Asha. Kobi was momentarily reminded of the attack by the rats in the transit tunnel beneath Old Seattle. This time though, Fionn stood apart, watching on, motionless.

Kobi had no time to think, but his body automatically braced to fight, hands reaching high to protect his face. His last hope was that if he killed enough of the rats with his bare hands they might retreat. He rushed in front of Asha, who was shouting something. As the rats leaped up toward him, he let out a primal scream.

The river of rodents broke apart at the last moment, streaming in two channels around their feet, before coalescing once more and making for Fionn.

"No!" screamed Asha, reaching out in terror.

The rats sprang onto Fionn's body, climbing his legs and spreading over his torso. The whole time he stood his ground, arms stretched out, as the creatures covered him completely, up his neck and through his hair, leaving only his face clear. At any moment, Kobi expected him to buckle as they bit into his skin, but Fionn was unperturbed. Serene, even, his eyes fixed on Asha. The rats stilled, perching across his limbs or clinging with their claws to his clothes, snouts twitching.

"Fionn, you're controlling them," Asha said, as if convincing herself about what she was seeing. She looked simultaneously horrified and in awe. Kobi shared the feeling: Fionn had never been this powerful before.

Fionn shook his head with a flash of anger that made Kobi hold his breath. *"Not controlling. Communicating."*

"It's . . . amazing," said Asha. "Like they're part of you. To be able to project to every single one of them . . . It's impressive, Fionn. I'll give you that."

Fionn smiled, looking for a second like the young boy Kobi remembered, shy and kindhearted.

"They're my friends."

Kobi watched as the rats descended, as if of one mind, scurrying off into the darkness.

"Waste must be getting down here," said Kobi. "A lot of it." *Mischik needs to know.* But how would Fionn react to that? They needed to tread lightly.

Fionn nodded and a ghost of a smile flickered over his lips. He fingered the wolf tooth and pointed the flashlight farther into the tunnel. *"Follow."*

He began to walk off.

Kobi caught Asha's eye and tapped his own head. He felt the telltale prickle as she read his thoughts: *We can't tell Fionn that this Waste contamination needs to be wiped out.*

They wandered back up the tunnel, Fionn leading the way. He moved with ease, even when the ceiling height dipped. Back at the rubble-strewn shaft, Asha stopped, touching her head in pain again.

"It's coming from down there."

Kobi joined her. "What is?"

"The strong feeling. Waste. Lots of it."

"More rats?"

Asha shook her head and turned to Fionn. "*Stay behind me,*" he said. "*I'll keep you safe.*" He seemed excited, like now that his secret had been discovered he was desperate to show it all off. *"Don't tell Mischik, all right?"*

Kobi caught Asha's eye again. "We won't," said Asha.

Dread settled in the pit of Kobi's stomach. He had a bad feeling: his instincts told him danger was close.

As they descended once more, through junctions and shafts, splashing occasionally through small pools of water, Kobi realized he hadn't been marking arrows on the walls, but Fionn seemed to know exactly where he was going. *I hope so. Otherwise we're completely lost. . . .*

"We must have walked miles by now," said Asha.

"I think we could be under the central district of the city," said Kobi. "You can feel the ground shake a bit from the traffic."

Dim light came from ahead, around a corner, but it didn't trouble Fionn at all. As they came closer, Kobi saw it wasn't a single source but a number of glowing points dancing in the air.

"Fireflies!" said Asha.

Fionn held up his hand as they approached, and the insects parted, forming into two distinct swarms that hovered on either side of them.

"That's incredible!" said Asha.

"*Down here, everything is my friend,*" said Fionn. He pointed and the fireflies drifted ahead, lighting the way. Kobi couldn't help but smile.

He heard water once more, at first just a few drips and a splash, then something louder. Under his feet, outlined in the fireflies' light, the base of the tunnel was softer, covered with patches of moss. How anything could grow down here in the dark was a mystery. Didn't plants need sunlight?

Asha, just ahead at the corner, suddenly stopped, her eyes wide.

"*Be careful,*" said Fionn.

Kobi reached them—and couldn't believe what he was seeing.

The tunnel floor had disintegrated completely. It simply ended in what looked like midair, and beyond, a huge cavern, larger even than the old football field at Bill Gates High School, stretched away. Waterfalls flooded from points near its ceiling, spouting into the space below, where they gathered in a pool covered in giant purple lily pads. Walls teeming with green plant life and phosphorescent flowers lined the cavern's perimeter, and moths the size of Kobi's head wafted gently through the air. But the weirdest thing of all was how it all *moved*. The plant life shifted and reached, seeming almost to grow before their eyes. It was beautiful but somehow menacing at the same time—a giant living organism.

And, without any doubt, a concentration of Waste of a kind Kobi hadn't seen since he'd left Old Seattle.

But this wasn't Old Seattle. This was beneath the new city—Kobi wondered how far they'd traveled underground. Had they moved from under the slums to the central district? Fionn's eyes gleamed as one of the moths fluttered closer, then landed on his outstretched hand. Fionn caught Kobi's eye, and Kobi was reminded of the butterfly shadow puppet Fionn had projected when they were staying at Bill Gates High School in Old Seattle—a Waste-mutated creature that wasn't evil or dangerous but to Fionn symbolized the beauty and freedom of the Wastelands. More than any other place, Old Seattle had been a home to him. He'd even spoken out loud there after having spent five years mute—the effects of a traumatizing CLAWS experiment in which he'd failed to control a mutated bear, allowing it to get loose and then kill a number of scientists before the young boy's eyes.

Kobi peeled his gaze from the butterfly, setting his look on Fionn. "We have to tell Mischik," he said.

The moth detached from Fionn's arm as the boy rounded on Kobi, eyes flashing. *"No!"*

"Fionn," Asha said, reaching for him. "You have to understand—this could be deadly. If this contamination reaches ground level, it'll be unstoppable. The Waste will consume New Seattle."

Kobi couldn't read Fionn's expression at all. *Perhaps he doesn't think that's a bad thing.* . . . "People will die, Fionn," he said. "Thousands of people."

Fionn's mouth tightened. "*I won't let that happen*," he said.

"You can't stop it," said Asha. "You might be able to control a few rats, but you can't—"

Fionn touched his temples, and it was like someone turned off the lights. The flowers seemed to lose their brightness, the fireflies faded, and all the plants that had been shifting and reaching and probing suddenly drooped. The water still flowed, crashing into the pool below, but otherwise everything was completely still.

"*Can't I?*" said Fionn. He turned to them, his face pleading. *"If you tell Sol, they'll want to destroy it all. That's all they know. Waste is bad. Kill the Waste. It's not fair."*

Asha was ready to argue, Kobi thought, but she simply sighed. "Okay, Fionn. We can talk about this, but you have to come back to base. If you don't, Sol will come looking anyway—they might even send drones down here. And they'll find this place."

Fionn looked defeated. Sulkily, he nodded, and pushed back past them. As he left, the lights of the jungle came alive once more. With a final look at the seething morass of vegetation, Kobi followed. He wondered how far underground they were and how high the Waste life had spread. There might be patches that had already reached the foundations of the soaring skyscrapers of New Seattle, waiting just below the streets.

When they reached the ladder up to the manhole, Fionn hung back.

"It's all right," said Kobi. "It's just the base."

There was a grim set to Fionn's shoulders, but he gripped the rungs and climbed.

They emerged back behind the generators and Kobi took a deep breath. The air wasn't fresh here by any means, but after being in the claustrophobic tunnels for the last couple of hours it tasted good. Fionn looked completely out of place, grubby and wild.

Asha smiled and ruffled his hair. "You need a shower!" she said.

"Not so fast," said a voice.

From behind the generator, Mischik stepped out, along with a Sol security detail. All of them were armed.

Fionn staggered back, right into Kobi.

"It's all right," said Asha, holding her ground. "It's just Dr. Mischik." She turned to the Sol personnel. "We just found Fionn," she said. "Is there a problem?"

Mischik's voice wavered as if he'd just experienced a shock. "We know you've been in the prohibited tunnels. You're still wearing your lenses, remember."

Kobi was confused. "They're switched off."

Mischik shook his head. "When we realized you were missing, we switched them back on."

"We saw everything," added the tall, bearded Sol agent who'd been riding Leon's motorbike during the mission to the clinic. His jaw was set.

Fionn began to shake his head rapidly. Kobi heard his voice in his head, though he knew Mischik and the others, who weren't infected, couldn't. *"Please don't hurt them. You can't kill it all!"*

"Get Fionn cleaned up," said Mischik. "Give him and Asha a strong dose of Horizon to flush their systems."

Fionn tried to run back down the tunnel, but the Sol staff rushed forward and grabbed him. Fionn thrashed and wailed.

"Keep him in his room until he calms down. Fionn, please, you have to understand," Mischik urged a little more gently.

The tall Sol agent pulled the boy away. Fionn looked back at Asha and Kobi with a quiet fury. *He blames us*, thought Kobi.

"Fionn, I'm sorry," said Asha, following after them. "We couldn't have known they were watching. It will be all right." With a last glance back at Kobi, Mischik turned after them, leaving Kobi alone.

Kobi took the lenses from his eyes, and tossed them away. He paced away toward the labs. A feeling of uneasiness welled in his stomach, and one thought wouldn't leave his brain, swirling around over and over. *The Waste in the tunnels won't be able to be contained. Waste is coming into the city. And it's going to be worse than ever.*

7

IN THE MEDICAL WING, Johanna was using a scanner to assess Kobi's vital organs. The device looked like a metal wand and gave readings as she moved it over his torso and head.

"Blood pressure fine—better, actually. Metabolism strong, levels of antibodies up." Her fingers elongated into vines and carried the device over Kobi's shoulders and down his back. "White blood cell production up too." She sighed. "You seem healthier than ever."

"I feel better than ever too. Just like back in . . ." He trailed off before he said, "*Old Seattle*."

But Johanna gave him a long stare, her auburn eyes as deep and rich as ferns. "I know what you're thinking."

Kobi looked away. "It's almost like I miss it. Waste. I miss being around it."

Johanna sat down beside him. "You think your abilities are

stronger because you have recently been exposed to Waste?"

Kobi didn't say anything for a moment. "It's possible, isn't it? I haven't felt right since I've been here, and it explains why I'm not as strong anymore, why you can't take as much blood. All of it. Fionn might be right. Me and him. We just don't belong here."

Johanna shook her head. "I don't agree with you." She picked up a tablet from a wheeled metallic table and sat back down. "I've been recording all of the Healhome kids' abilities." She touched the tablet a few times, bringing up a set of graphs with the names of each Healhome kid on a graph's axis. Kobi saw quickly that only his baseline measurements were down. Fionn's graph showed a sharp increase, Asha's a slight upward curve, and Johanna's graph had dramatically increased since the date of their arrival six months ago.

She pointed to hers. "I think our abilities run far deeper and are far more complex than we know. I think training helps them grow, but I also think the powers depend on our mental state—on the connection between our body and mind. And what triggers their development is different for all of us. Fionn's powers have skyrocketed since we arrived here. I think his powers are fueled by *anger*. By feeling in control. You've seen the change in him."

She extended her fingers into a twirling column. "I think my powers have developed because I feel useful. I have found what I'm good at." Kobi studied her face and saw a lingering sadness. "At Healhome I never fit in. I wasn't loud or strong or determined. I never felt like part of the group. It was only really Rohan that I was friends with. He was always kind and so funny. I miss him." She paused. "I think I've found *purpose*."

Kobi heard Hales's voice in his head again, pictured his face suddenly, and felt himself droop as if pulled down by a great weight. "I miss Hales too. I miss being with him. I miss my old life. I just don't think I can be strong without him. Maybe my powers are linked to that somehow?"

Johanna smiled sadly at him. "You have to find what you're missing, what's holding you back."

An alarm cut through the room, a sharp wail from the corridor. Johanna stood, rigid. "It's the emergency alert. Doctors are being called in."

A surge of dread filled Kobi instantly. "Rohan!"

Together Kobi and Johanna rushed from the testing room, picking their way through the crowded main atrium until they located the passage that led to the makeshift medical room. When they arrived, Kobi saw that the glass partition had misted and doctors crowded inside. The door was automated, and Kobi didn't have clearance. He thought about kicking it in.

"I'll open it," called Johanna. She pressed her finger on a light blue scanner pad, and the door whistled open. "Kobi, wait!" said Johanna, but he pushed through the doctors until he could see the bed.

Rohan was having some kind of seizure. His body twisted and jerked. A bald male doctor with pale freckled skin held him down by the shoulders.

"Cardiac arrest," said a tall, dark-skinned woman with short gray hair—clearly in charge. "Steve, the defibrillator." She opened Rohan's gown at the chest. Kobi was ushered back by a nurse.

A third doctor, eyes steely, placed two electrical cathodes on either side of Rohan's heart. "Clear!" said the head doctor.

Rohan's body leaped from the bed.

"Still no heartbeat," said a nurse by a machine Kobi couldn't identify.

"Clear!" said the head doctor again. Rohan's body spasmed, but his eyes remained closed. Kobi couldn't look at his face. The slack cheeks and lifeless skin were too much for Kobi to bear. "No. Rohan, no," whispered Kobi, his shoulders and arms frozen into leaden, sinking weights. The room seemed to spin.

The doctors administered the shocks to his heart another time, then another, then another, until Kobi saw them slowing, casting doubtful looks at each other. The lead doctor glanced over to where Johanna and Kobi were watching frozen near the doorway. Kobi could read everything he needed to know in her gaze. But he couldn't accept it.

"Keep going," said Kobi, and he heard Johanna burst out in sobs.

Mischik strode into the room. The doctor shook her head at the Sol leader. "Rohan didn't make it. Cardiac arrest caused by the toxin."

Mischik opened his mouth, but he wavered. No words escaped him. Finally, he swallowed and put his hands on Kobi and Johanna's shoulders. "He's gone. Rohan's gone."

"No," whispered Kobi. The doctors moved away and, as if watching himself from afar, Kobi walked in a daze to Rohan's side, touching the soft skin of his arm. He was so still now. Johanna followed him, then bent and kissed Rohan on the cheek.

"No," said Kobi. It was all he could say.

Kobi told Leon the news himself. He thought it would be best coming from him. But it was undoubtedly the hardest thing Kobi had ever had to do. Leon had broken down completely, curling up on the sofa in the game room with his hands over his face and wailing. He'd gone to see Rohan's body, and two hours later, he still hadn't come back. Kobi, Yaeko, Asha, and Fionn sat in the game room in silence. Kobi could sense the grief spreading in waves from Fionn. The last time Fionn had seen Rohan, his friend had been healthy. Asha had filled him in on their mission to the anti-Waste clinic in the slums, and the attack from the Snatchers. Fionn had listened with tears in his eyes. *"I should have been there with you. I shouldn't have disappeared. I could have helped."*

Kobi looked up and saw Johanna enter the turbine hall. "Kobi, Asha, can I have a word?" she said.

When they were outside, Johanna cast a look around, then whispered, "I want to show you something." Her eyes were puffy and worn out. Kobi just nodded, too tired to ask any questions. Asha must have felt the same because she followed wordlessly alongside Kobi. Johanna led them down a couple of levels to the storage facilities. The rest of the base was a hive of activity, though it seemed somehow muted. Word had got around of the contamination beneath the city. A pall of despair and desperation seeped into every corridor, every set of eyes, palpable in the slumped body language, the muttered voices. Rohan had been popular. His death seemed like an omen for the end. *We're losing*, thought Kobi. *Everyone knows it.*

Johanna's fingerprint gave them access to a small storage room. It contained the smells of damp and dust, like it wasn't used very much. *Strange that the door is still secure though*, Kobi thought. *What's in here*? The room seemed ordinary, lined with shelves and plastic crates. Johanna reached toward one of the upper shelves. She wrapped leaflike tendrils around a small box. Opening the lid, she took out a battered drone. Kobi recognized it. He'd seen one of this kind before. Kobi's skin tingled, and he breathed in a sharp gasp. *It can't be.*

"I should have shown you this before," she said, "but Mischik made me swear not to. I caught him watching the drone footage in his quarters. He didn't know I was there at first. I don't even know if anyone else has seen the recording."

Kobi held his breath as Johanna switched on the drone. A projected head appeared, and Kobi's heart rattled in response. It was Jonathan Hales. His features were tired and drawn, indicating prolonged Waste exposure. He looked close to collapse.

"Play message," said Johanna.

"G*reetings, Alex*," Hales said in a weak voice. He began to cough, and his words tumbled out in a disjointed ramble. *"I . . . I have had a breakthrough. I didn't want to say until I was sure"*—more coughing—*"but I fear I may not have long left. I've stayed here too long already."* He lifted a piece of paper into the shot. *"I found something. It was in Apana's office in a secret compartment. I don't think he trusted anyone. You know what he was like. It always had to be about him. Anyway, I discovered the key to completing the cure. We have the cleansers, but this—this is the key to eradicating the Waste permanently! And I know where to go. The Park site! It's going to be difficult to get there, impossible for me—for everyone—but there is one person who can do it. Kobi!"*

Hales took a deep breath, as if wrestling with some internal battle. *"He's still only thirteen, Alex, but . . . I know he could."* He paused. *"It's time to come clean with him, Alex. I . . . I don't know how he'll take it. I've lied to him his whole life. He thinks I'm his dad—and I am in a way. He's my son, but he won't see that. He won't understand. I know it."* Hales seemed lost in his own thoughts, but then his head jerked to one side, eyes widening. *"There's something out there. . . . . Oh my god . . . Alex, Snatchers!"* His face came closer to the camera, and the room behind him spun. *"Alex, I don't have long. Kobi needs help. He's on his own. Get him out of here. He's the only—"*

The message ended.

For a long time, nobody spoke, until at last Johanna bent down, replaced the drone in the box, then lifted it back onto the shelf.

"He must have launched the drone just before he was captured," she said.

He was going to tell me the truth, Kobi thought. For a moment, he let himself imagine if Hales had made it back from the lab. How different things could have been.

"What's the Park site?" asked Asha.

"I don't know," said Kobi. "I need to look at the map. Something about it sounds familiar, but I can't remember. . . ." A mix of emotions raged inside him. His chest felt tight with pain at seeing Hales alive again, his last moments captured on a screen. But there was a new drive, too, burning inside: everything seemed clearer now. *He believed in me. He said I was the only one who could do it.* "I'm going back to the Wastelands. I'm going to find the Park site."

Asha spoke in a quick, urgent tone, locking him with a firm stare. "You can't, Kobi. You can't go out there on your own."

"Exactly," said Kobi, "which is why I'll need help."

Asha's lips parted as she realized what he was asking. "I'll go with you," she said, "but we'll need Fionn too."

Johanna shook her head. "Mischik won't let you go," she said.

"Then we won't ask for his permission," Kobi said. "I have to trust in my dad."

Asha looked startled. Kobi had called Hales his dad. He hadn't done that since he'd found out the truth. But Kobi realized now: Hales had been his father in a way, whether Kobi liked it or not. He had raised him, nurtured him—and he had loved him. Kobi could see that love in the video, but he had felt it his entire life.

"Mischik is doing his best," said Johanna, still looking at the frozen, glowing image of Hales's terrified face. "But he doesn't have the answers. We've got Waste closing in from below, CLAWS from above. It's a matter of time. But Mischik just can't see it."

"Let's get the others," said Kobi.

Asha frowned. "You think we should all go?"

Kobi nodded. "We're all Wastelings. We belong together."

Asha smiled. "Wastelings? Sounds like something Rohan would say."

Kobi nodded. "Yeah, it does—it's what we'd be called in one of his superhero comics."

"Or the name for our baseball team. The Wastelings," Asha replied.

"I'll get Leon," said Johanna. "He'll be with Rohan. You two go get Fionn and Yaeko."

As they slipped out from the storage room, making their way back to the game room, Kobi kept glancing up at the cameras angled down at the corridors; he felt suddenly aware of how many there were.

Fionn was playing on a VR headset, and Yaeko was watching a reality TV show. Leon turned up a minute later with Johanna. His eyes were rimmed with red. "What's this about, Caveman?" he said. His voice sounded hoarse from crying. "I want to get back to Rohan."

"We're leaving," Kobi announced. There were gasps from

the others. "And you're all coming with me. If you want to." He explained what they'd found out about the cure, already finished by Hales, out there somewhere in the Wastelands. Leon shifted in his chair, looking baffled. Yaeko just whistled.

"When do we leave?" Fionn's face blazed with happiness.

"Soon," Kobi told him. "We'll go soon."

"We'll need a way out," said Asha. "I don't think Mischik will just fling open the door for us."

"I might be able to help with that," said Johanna. "I've got clearance for the doors. I can get you out. We need to plan though. Old Seattle is a hundred miles west over the mountains—and the land between us is scorched by incinerator drones to stop the spread of Waste. You'll need to know the schedule of the drone sweeps. I might be able to get that. I know that Mischik has some contact with smugglers who travel there."

"Thanks, Johanna. What do you say, Leon?"

"I . . . I don't know."

Kobi stared at him. "Aren't you excited to finally do something? To take the fight to CLAWS?"

"I was," he said. His voice was hollow. "But sure, I'll come. Why not?" He turned away, hunched in an armchair as he watched the holo-TV.

Kobi met Yaeko's eye. "We could use you out there too." Leon snorted, not looking over. Kobi ignored him. "The only way we stand a chance is if we stick together."

"We're the Wastelings," said Asha. "We were born from the

Waste, and we are the ones who have to end it." She smiled. "It sounds like our baseball team name, right? The Wastelings. Rohan never could find one." The boy grunted something back.

Yaeko rubbed her jaw, then shrugged. "Sure, I'm in too. But FYI, chances are this is going to fail. Maybe some mutated freak-azoid bear or eagle or whatever makes tofu out of us. Or we get picked up by CLAWS. Or if we're really lucky, we die a slow, painful death from Waste poisoning. We're not all one hundred percent immune like you, Kobi."

"I'll get cleansers for you to take with you," said Johanna. "You don't need to worry."

"Okay. Thanks, Jo. I'll stop worrying," said Yaeko.

Kobi turned to the bark-skinned girl. "Aren't you coming?"

Johanna returned his imploring gaze with a gentle shake of her head. "I don't belong out there. I'm not like the rest of you. I'm not brave." She smiled as Kobi tried to protest. "It's okay. I belong in the labs. I know that. I'll do everything I can to help the cause from here. And I'll keep Sol off your back."

Kobi nodded. Johanna stepped forward and hugged him. "Find the cure. Find it for Rohan."

8

KOBI SAT ON HIS bed, staring at the map of Old Seattle. His eyes flitted between the many *L*s representing Hales's labs scattered across the city. Asha sat next to him. Kobi felt the prickling over his skull as she listened to his thoughts. The camera watched from above. Sol would be suspicious if Kobi removed the map from his room, so he'd decided to examine it here. He could communicate with Asha telepathically, and the camera wouldn't pick up their exchange.

The "Park site" has to be one of these labs, he thought slowly and carefully so Asha could catch every word. She met his eye and gave a subtle nod. *I thought I'd seen it before on this map, but there are no parks around any of Hales's labs. I don't get it.*

His eyes drifted to the *L* drawn over Mercer Island, east of the main Seattle island, separated from the rest of the city by Lake Washington. It had been a wealthy district, full of the mansions of the super-rich with their own private quays to keep their yachts. Kobi had never seen the island, even from a distance. Mercer Island had been the epicenter of the explosion of Waste in the city. It was the most contaminated place in the world.

Wait . . . Give me your phone. Asha frowned and handed it to him. "Search Apana Park," Kobi told it. He glanced up at the camera. To anyone watching, it wouldn't look like Kobi and Asha were doing anything suspicious; just some innocent research into the original Waste outbreak. It was natural Kobi would be interested. Sol wouldn't understand the real reason behind his internet search. He pressed on a video labeled, "Apana Park launch commercial, June 2022." As the video began to play, Kobi said, "Holo-mode." A beam of light displayed the video in 3D a few inches above the tablet.

A bearded man wearing circular spectacles paced through a pristine lab. Scientists worked all around him, peering into microscopes and arranging racks of test tubes. "Do you want to watch history being made?" the man asked. He stopped, smiling a toothy grin. "I'm Alan Apana, head of GrowCycle. Seattle, I invite you to witness a new dawn for humanity: the launch of a product that will revolutionize the world. GAIA!"

The image switched to a beautiful garden with large healthy trees and vegetables and fruits growing at a visible rate in a plot. The stems stretched and separated, spawning buds that quickly expanded into leaves, producing tomatoes, strawberries ripening and enlarging to full size in a matter of seconds, like something recorded with a time-lapse capture camera. Apana, now dressed in shorts and a T-shirt, sat in a lawn chair in the shade of a large apple tree. "This is my garden." He stood up and plucked an apple from a low tree, taking a bite. The camera remained on the branch as another fruit began to swell in its place. He swallowed, giving a thumbs-up. "Using GAIA, I created this garden from seedlings over the course of only a few hours. Imagine this on a world scale: crops that can be grown and then harvested the same day. Imagine hunger solved. Imagine a world where starvation and famine are things of the past."

The camera panned to a wall of giant hedges surrounding the garden. "Imagine trees that cleanse the air of pollution at a rate previously thought impossible. Imagine an unlimited source of biofuel—a solution for the energy crisis!" He reached down and picked up a canister labeled "GAIA," with a logo in the shape of a globe. "This is my gift to you." The picture switched to a sweeping shot of a huge field of cleared, ploughed earth. GrowCycle-branded drones hovered above it. "Thanks to a high concentration of GAIA, it will take only a few *seconds* for this field to grow into a wondrous botanical garden—Apana Park."

Kobi turned excitedly to Asha, whose eyes were wide.

The Park site, Asha—Apana Park, Kobi said to her inside his head. *It's on Mercer Island. There must be an old GrowCycle lab there.*

The GrowCycle commerical was still playing. Apana stood in the middle of the ploughed field, staring up at the camera with his arms wide as the shot expanded. When the camera had zoomed out enough, letters appeared in the form of trees shooting up from the soil: a teaser of what the lucky spectactors would witness at the big launch of Apana Park. The foliage spelled out the GrowCycle slogan: "GrowCycle. Nourishing Humanity."

"Off," Kobi snapped, and the projection vanished.

"Do you think GAIA actually worked for a while?" Asha said. "Before it went wrong? That garden looked pretty convincing."

"I bet it was just CGI," said Kobi. "That was just a commercial, a way to convince people to buy GAIA. I think he was as bad as CLAWS at misleading people."

Kobi wished he could warn them all, everyone who had been drawn in by that video and made plans to go to the launch. The smiling figure of Apana and the fake, glossy quality of the commerical made Kobi seethe with anger. The reality of the Waste had been nothing like that, nothing but destruction, suffering, and death—including the death of Apana himself. "I wish Apana had survived," said Kobi, voice hard and sharp. "So he could see what he'd done."

Asha looked grim. "Me too. But it's up to us now, Kobi. We need to put it right."

"It's time," said Johanna in the game room later that evening. "There's a room near the manhole cover—I've cordoned off the whole area. I've left some supplies there, including enough Horizon to last all of you a couple of weeks." She turned to Kobi. "Except you, of course."

"Thanks, Jo," said Kobi. "We'll see you soon."

"You'd better," said Johanna, her eyes starting to well with tears. She stepped away. "No time for goodbyes. Just . . . go. And good luck."

They left her, slinking through the shadowy base, descending deeper. Yaeko took the lead, keeping herself disguised against the tunnel walls until she could give the all clear. But their route was quiet. They found the supplies in the room Johanna had mentioned: civilian clothing, first-aid kits, and food-packs, as well as flashlights and water flasks with built-in filters. Johanna had managed to scavenge a single stun baton plus utility tools, each equipped with a small knife. And most important of all, there were syringes filled with Horizon.

"Nice work, Johanna," said Asha.

They reached the corridor leading to the manhole entrance when alarms began to sound. Everyone froze.

"It must be Sol!" said Yaeko. "They know what we're doing."

"Run for it!" Leon shouted. They broke into a sprint along the passage. Kobi wondered how their secret could have gotten out.

But that didn't matter now. They ran ahead. But Kobi stopped suddenly when he heard shouts. Over his wrist communicator, he heard Mischik's voice. "Kobi! They're here! We need to get you out!" Kobi heard a mechanical whir he recognized all too well, making his blood chill to ice, and then a scream. He couldn't tell if it was Mischik or not.

"Snatchers," said Kobi. "CLAWS has found the base."

As he said it, he heard thuds above their head and scuttling from down the corridor.

"Oh god," said Yaeko, her skin rippling through different colors in her panic.

Kobi picked out a movement behind them in the gray scale of his night vision. The shimmer of long metal legs. As the Snatcher approached he felt a wave of terror pulse from Fionn.

"Johanna!" said Asha. "We need to go back and help her!"

"We can't," said Kobi. "We have to go, now!" His panic had cleared—a reaction to danger forged over his years in the Wastelands. He pulled out the stun baton, activated the charge.

He heard the dart coming. He swiveled and thrust up his backpack, and the dart exploded against it, smashing some vials of the Horizon inside, the leaking serum dampening the fabric. Kobi grimaced. *Come a little closer. . . .*

As soon as he saw the red eyes, Kobi fired the baton. Sparks exploded from the end, fizzing across the Snatcher's wiring. Its legs buckled. "Go!" yelled Kobi. The group raced down through the manhole. Kobi slammed it closed behind him.

"The Snatchers can't get through here, but we need to move fast." Kobi dropped down and forged ahead with a flashlight. His communicator came to life again, playing sounds of explosions and ricocheting gunfire. Screams. Shouts of pain, voices.

"We're being overrun!"

"We've got drones coming in through three tunnels."

"I don't think we can—"

"Evacuate! Emergency exits."

"Use the doors to block them off."

Kobi felt a tight pull in his gut. None of them was Mischik's voice. They were coming through on Mischik's channel, but Mischik himself wasn't saying anything.

Kobi thought of him lying dead or too injured to move. He thought of Spike, of all the Sol workers he didn't know. Johanna. He took off the watch and threw it to the ground, the bursts of voices and static fading in the dim, dripping passage behind them as they ran. He couldn't do anything to save them now.

"They have an evacuation plan in case the base is invaded," said Kobi. He was trying to reassure the others, but Kobi could see his own doubt reflected in their faces. No one else said anything.

9

THEY HURRIED FOR WHAT seemed like hours. They couldn't afford to rest. Kobi kept expecting Snatchers around every corner. He refused to let fatigue hinder his senses. He had the blueprints of the sewer network in his hand, illuminated by the beam of his flashlight. Yaeko kept asking how long before they reached the edge of the city.

"You asking isn't going to make us get there any sooner!" Asha finally snapped at her.

"If I'd known we were going to be down here for *eternity*," Yaeko replied, "I wouldn't have eaten my sandwich in one go. I don't know why Johanna thought I liked tuna salad." A heavy silence followed.

"She'll be okay," said Asha. "Either she escaped, or CLAWS will want as many people alive as possible. They'll want to question them."

Maybe they'll wish they hadn't been taken alive, Kobi thought, but kept it to himself.

Finally, Kobi directed them to the location Johanna had circled on the blueprints. Kobi climbed a rusted ladder and punched out a warped sewer grate above his head, emerging into a sparse, quiet area at the edge of the slums. They could see remnants of the old city of Wenatchee, which had mostly been leveled to build New Seattle: old-fashioned housing, motels, and highways broken into lumps of crumbling asphalt. The route of the old Columbia River, diverted for fear of contamination, scarred the soil, full of rubbish and a few makeshift camps.

Workers that Kobi guessed were on their way to the industrial farming facilities outside the city began to congregate around stalls selling coffee and food. Kobi and the others found the fruit pickers' stop easily enough and joined a herd of people waiting in line. Several showed signs of Waste deformities, and one middle-aged man didn't stop coughing, except to spit blood into the road. When the transport eventually came, it slowed but didn't stop, and workers filed onto it. The transport was open-topped, something between a train and a bus. Kobi and his friends climbed aboard the last car.

The transport joined a small highway of other such vehicles, all heading west. Intersections split off toward enormous hangars and warehouses, and they passed fields of gleaming solar panels and forests of spinning wind turbines. Kobi couldn't help but remember the tiny solar generator he and Hales had once relied on, barely enough to power the refrigerator and charge their flashlights. Occasional drones now zipped overhead, but they didn't look like Snatchers. Hopefully CLAWS wouldn't even think of looking for them all the way out here.

The sheer scale of the farms was astonishing, spreading out under the distant silhouettes of the mountains of the Okanogan-Wenatchee National Forest. The vehicle in which Kobi and the others were riding joined a procession of similar transports. There must have been thousands of workers, Kobi thought. Automated announcements read out various combinations of numbers and letters.

Kobi said nothing, and neither did the others. There was nothing to say. They just watched, enthralled, as the mass of the mountains loomed closer like the spine of some vast prehistoric monster.

At the last stop, the adults went toward a shed with a transparent plastic roof, scanning cards at the doorway, but Kobi and the others hung back and continued on foot. The road became rougher and emptier, coarse grass growing over skeletons of ancient, abandoned cars and trucks. They began to climb into the forested foothills on what must have been an old hiking trail, though it looked like no one had been this way for years. Kobi took the lead, feeling oddly at home away from the hard lines and industry of the city. These weren't the Waste-infected forests of Old Seattle but real, healthy trees. The smell of pine resin was rich in the air.

Kobi had never seen a wilderness that wasn't full of Waste. It was so peaceful.

Yaeko and Leon walked close together, marveling at the soaring trunks. Kobi realized they'd probably never seen anything like them in their lives. Plants at Healhome had been potted and pruned, and there was nothing like these in the slums.

"Amazing, isn't it?" said Kobi.

"At least the trees here don't try to kill you," said Asha.

Only Fionn looked unimpressed. *"Boring."*

Yaeko ran her fingers along one of the trunks, and her fingers momentarily took on the dark hues of the bark, seeming to blend with the wood. They looked just like Johanna's. When Yaeko saw him watching, her skin blinked back to normal. *She tries to hide it, but she's just as upset about Johanna as we are.*

When a stream cut across their path, Kobi and Leon pushed over a dead oak and together carried it and toppled it over the water to make a bridge. "Too easy," Kobi said to Leon.

"Nothing to it. Not for the Caveman." The tall boy gave a half-hearted smile that quickly faded. Since Rohan's death, it was like the life had been sucked out of him.

They emerged from the forest after a couple of hours and stopped for a break on a scrubby plateau. Kobi was amazed how far they'd come already. The crop fields were far below, and in the distance New Seattle bristled in the sunlight. The slums, climbing to the north, were an ugly mound. More drones than he'd ever seen were patrolling the skies above.

Asha came to his side. "D'you think anyone made it out? Really?"

"I hope so," he replied. "But if CLAWS got their hands on the Horizon drugs, I'm sure they destroyed it all. If we fail now, the resistance is finished."

A weight pressed down on Kobi as he said the words. *How did this happen to me?* he wondered, struck with a disorienting sense of disbelief. "Not long ago, I only had to worry about keeping myself and Hales alive. Now we have to protect the entire human race." He met Asha's gaze.

"Easy peasy," she said, and they both laughed.

They trekked late into the day. As the foliage thickened to dense forest, the calls of animals began shrill against the setting sun. Fionn ran ahead. After about ten minutes, they heard his voice projected into their minds. *"Come here!"*

Fionn was sitting on the ground, grinning, in front of a pine cone as big as a football. Kobi looked up and saw other cones weighing down the sagging branches. His heart sank. He'd seen some large ones earlier, but this was clearly not natural.

"There must be Waste here," said Asha. "Maybe this is where it's getting into the city from—the water runoff from the mountains is getting into the tunnels under the city. I thought the point of the Scorched Lands was to prevent the airborne spores crossing from Old Seattle. Waste needs to be carried by fungi and plants to spread, right? And animals, though I guess the desert can't stop birds and insects just flying here if they can dodge the incinerator drones."

Leon frowned. "Do you think CLAWS is monitoring it?"

"They must be. They just don't care," said Yaeko.

Kobi surveyed the trees. Some were still normal, but others had branches that were swollen and twisted out of shape. The familiar mutations brought a pang to his chest. He realized he had almost *missed* the sight of a natural Waste environment. But he knew also how dangerous it was that the contamination was so close to the city. If animals were getting across the Scorched Lands and spreading Waste, why wasn't CLAWS doing anything about it? They could have drones out here spraying insecticide, and targeting airborne mutated creatures. The answer came clear to him. How could he be so stupid?

"It's not that they don't care," said Kobi, his voice growing loud with anger. "I think they *want* some Waste in the city. It keeps everyone scared and raises the demand for their drugs." The more he thought about it, the more he was sure he was right. "But they can't control it. They think they can, but they can't. The Waste always finds a way to spread. It can't be contained."

Asha and Kobi exchanged a look. He guessed her thoughts also had honed in on the forest of Waste that lay in wait beneath the city. CLAWS had created that. Kobi was stuck in an overwhelming wave of the extent of the scope for evil CLAWS had.

"They'll pay for what they've done," said Asha, placing a hand on Kobi's shoulder. "We'll make sure they pay."

* * *

The landscape on the other side of the mountains was all black. A steep, lifeless desert, like the surface of another planet. The trees were charred stumps. The vehicles on the melted road looked like rusting shells.

"The Scorched Lands," said Asha. "Name checks out."

"I wouldn't come here on my vacation," said Yaeko. "But I've never had a vacation. So I wouldn't know."

Kobi stared at the devastation—not a single tree or building or animal. "The old city is on the other side somewhere," he said.

"Past the incinerator drones?" said Yaeko. "Those sound fun."

"Johanna got us the schedule," said Kobi, drawing out from his bag a map with different zones and lists of patrol times.

"Is it accurate?" asked Yaeko.

"Let's hope so," said Kobi.

Leon just shook his head, his eyes fixed in horror at the endless burned terrain. "We don't have to do this," he said. "We could turn back."

"To CLAWS?" said Asha.

"To somewhere else," said Leon, his expression hardening. "Not New Seattle. That place is doomed, right? But we could go to another city. Rohan always wanted to travel. Spike talked about other places that are Waste free."

"That's just avoiding the problem," said Asha. "Waste free for how long?"

"I'll take those chances," said Leon. "When New Seattle gets filled with Waste, people will turn on CLAWS anyway. We just need to wait it out."

Kobi felt a lightness spread in his chest. "CLAWS would be ruined. No one would ever trust them again. Maybe then Sol could reemerge. We could use Horizon to cure people, spread it to the world without CLAWS getting in the way."

Leon nodded. "They brought this on themselves."

"No, Kobi," said Asha, shaking her head at him. "We can't let all those people die. It would be like Old Seattle all over again—thousands and thousands of lives. We're not CLAWS. We can't let innocent people die."

Kobi closed his eyes shut for a moment, letting out a deep sigh. "You're right. I know. It's just . . . Jo, Mischik, Hales. All those people CLAWS let die to keep them in business. Finally, people would see them for what they are."

Yacko cocked her head at him. "Come on, Caveman. We all know you aren't going to let that happen. You like being a hero too much."

Kobi didn't bother to protest. He felt the weight of responsibility falling heavily on him once more. For just a moment he had dared to hope that it all didn't rest on him, but that was all it was: a hope.

He remembered the message from Hales. *"There is one person who could make it."*

"I can't turn back."

Leon pointed at the black landscape. "Look out there—you

really think we'll find answers out there?"

Kobi didn't want to look at the others because he was scared of what he might see in their faces. He wouldn't blame them if they wanted to turn back now.

"I'm with Kobi," said Asha. Kobi felt a surge of gratitude. "We've come this far. We owe it to Sol."

"I don't owe them anything," said Leon. "They let Rohan die."

"*I'm with Kobi too,*" said Fionn.

"Okay, consider this," said Leon. "If you make it to another city, they'll have scientists too. Who says they won't be able to synthesize your blood and create better medicines?"

"CLAWS would try and stop us," said Kobi.

"We can keep you safe," said Leon.

"We couldn't even keep Rohan safe," said Asha. "CLAWS won't stop hunting us."

Yaeko stepped toward Leon. "You were right. It was my fault, what happened to Rohan. So if I can make things right I will. And that means going with Kobi."

Leon folded his arms. "Suit yourselves," he said, "but the Waste has taken my whole life so far. This is where I stop."

Kobi looked at his stony expression and saw there was no way he could make Leon change his mind.

"Where will you go?" Kobi asked.

Leon shrugged. "Back to the bus stop, I guess. Then find a train out of New Seattle and down the coast. I heard Hollywood is clean."

"They'll be looking for you," said Yaeko.

"They're looking for Kobi," said Leon.

The words stung Kobi, but he kept his words calm. "I won't force you. Any of you." *Rohan would have come*, thought Kobi. But it seemed like something had died in Leon too when his best friend succumbed to the Snatcher's toxin.

"I'm not a hero," said Leon. "I never asked to be." Kobi's heart sank as he watched his friend trudge away and not look back.

I never asked to be either, Kobi thought.

10

THE ROLLING HILLS OF black desert were a constant presence on either side of the freeway. Each step kicked up clouds of ash and charcoal. The air tasted thick, filled with particles of unseen dust. They took out spare T-shirts that Johanna had packed for them and tied them around their noses and mouths. Still, when the wind gusted, it snatched up black clouds, and they were forced to turn away or take shelter until the ash storm passed.

"We're safe on this route for another hour," Kobi shouted into the choking wind, "then we need to head east to avoid the Scorcher drone!"

Forty miles to go, Kobi thought, reading the map. *Today and tonight and we should be there.* He was gripped with a sense of guilt. If he was on his own he could run it in a third of the time, and the risk from the incinerator drones would be reduced. Was he right in bringing the others with him? It wasn't too late to send them off after Leon, away from danger. But he had to believe in his gut. It was the oldest rule and the simplest.

"Trust your instincts, Kobi."

And his instincts said that they were stronger as a team.

But as they carried on, doubt curdled in the back of his mind. What if they'd miscalculated? What if this was the wrong direction? There were no landmarks to measure by other than the contour lines showing elevation on the map, so he had to guess at distances. He kept the arc of the sun in mind. But drifting a mile either way could take them into the path of an incinerator drone.

Occasionally they talked, if only to check in or to share water. They rationed it to sips, but Kobi knew as they finished the first of their four flasks that the battle against dehydration would be as much of an obstacle as the distance. When they were halfway through their supply, they'd have to make a choice. The safe option: turn back. The other: push on.

As evening began to spread its cloak over the endless, burned landscape, Kobi began to notice the silence. It hadn't been obvious when it was light. But usually twilight brought animals, perhaps a cool wind rustling the trees, the buzz of insects. Out here there was nothing. The silence itself seemed like a continual background hum in his ears.

"Can you hear that?" said Asha. Kobi saw her watching him in the dark. Kobi listened. "In the distance." Then he heard it. There was a hum washing through the silent open landscape. So faint it was almost imperceptible. But as they trudged on, and he honed in on the sound, he noticed slight changes in its frequency.

"Scorchers." He tapped his map. "They're close." He pointed into the distance as a haze of orange spread through the sky, sweeping closer until it blazed perhaps only a mile from their position.

"If we're going to be incinerated, don't bother letting me know," said Yaeko, dark eyes like jewels in the fiery light.

"*Me neither,*" came a voice in Kobi's head, and he could tell Fionn had projected it to the other two as well because Yaeko grinned.

"Let's hope it doesn't come to that," said Asha. "But you know what, don't tell me either."

"Got it," Kobi said.

Above, the stars shone like brilliant eyes in the pure black sky. To draw his attention from the cascading hum and deadly glare of the nearby scorchers, Kobi named the constellations, hearing Hales's voice pointing them out.

"That's Taurus, son, the bull. And that's Orion, the great hunter. The Greeks believed he was never seen in the sky with Scorpio, the scorpion, because he was running from it. The scorpion's sting killed the hunter when he showed too much hubris. Gemini, the twins. Aries, the ram. The compass—that one can only be seen in the summer months. Sirius, omen of death, near Thuban, there, which was once the North Star in ancient times. The night sky changes over the centuries. Right now our North Star is there—exactly at the pole. Pretty useful if you need to know where you're going."

The North Star, second brightest in the sky, now flickered like a distant boat, light in a black ocean. Kobi kept it to their right-hand side.

"We've been going for four hours," said Asha, checking her watch. The orange flare of distant Scorcher drones on the Horizon surrounded them now. It matched up to Kobi's map and schedule. Right now they were in the eye of the storm, in the only safe zone in a ten-mile radius.

"We should be able to see the old city at any minute," said Kobi.

"Are you sure we're going the right way?" asked Yaeko.

Asha gave her a look. "Thanks for the input, but if you wanted to help in orienting, maybe you could have offered your help a bit earlier? But who knows? Maybe Kobi's got it wrong, and we'll find ourselves in Hollywood with Leon."

"All right, jeez," said Yaeko. "I was just trying to help, but you know what? I'll just enjoy the scenery. Those incinerator drones are *so* pretty."

Kobi surveyed the Horizon. The paths of the drones remained at a safe distance. He allowed himself a brief moment of satisfaction that he had so far navigated the drones without any mistakes.

"Never take your situation for granted. Things can change in a second."

Kobi gave a small nod in reply and turned back to the map before Fionn's voice cut in.

"I can see something ahead."

Kobi spotted a line cutting across the terrain, like a perfectly even mountain range. The orange dawn sun peeped over it, casting rays into the bluish skyline like spotlights from a concert stage. "It's the wall."

"It's a *massive* wall," said Yaeko.

"Built to contain the Waste," said Asha. "It's part of the quarantine."

Kobi knew of it too, having read at the Sol base all he could about recent history. He'd been so shocked he'd almost laughed to learn that his entire former home had been contained within such a defined boundary. But now seeing it for himself, he felt only disbelief. "All my life, I was living inside that thing, and I had no idea."

"*How are we going to get over it?*" said Fionn.

"I don't know," said Kobi truthfully. "But let's just take things one step at a time."

"Well, I can climb it," said Yaeko. "As much as I'd love to wait with you until the Scorcher drones come." She flicked her gaze at Asha. "I am good for something." Asha rolled her eyes.

The wall grew in size as they approached. Kobi hadn't realized exactly how massive the scale would be; he guessed they were still miles away. He looked at his watch. *We have only an hour before the Scorcher drone is scheduled.* "We need to get moving."

They hurried on until the wall rose above them. It cast the desert in shadow. Kobi had the impression of a frozen tsunami about to crash over them. His skin itched. The concrete surface was scarred and pitted.

"Oh no." Fionn's voice filled Kobi's head with a jolt of fear. *"They're coming."*

Fionn was staring behind him. Kobi turned. There, like distant birds in the sky, came a fleet of incinerator drones. Their progress was a distant rumble, and they flew in perfect formation, descending serenely. Kobi counted fourteen of them, all heading in their direction. He checked the map again. The drones were arriving ahead of schedule. Perhaps the timings had been adjusted.

"They're coming sooner than I thought. Quick! We have to get to the wall!"

Kobi ran, but the others couldn't keep pace. The Scorchers were only a few hundred yards away when the sheets of fire began to fall from their bellies. The roar was deafening. As the flames hit the ground, smoke rose in great clouds behind them. Kobi knew they wouldn't make it. The wall was still too far away. Even if they reached the bottom, they had nowhere to hide. It was hopeless.

Flames filled the air. Kobi pressed his hands over his ears. The heat was coming in waves, and he knew it would only get worse. Everything was yellows and oranges. Yaeko threw herself to the ground and curled into a ball, and Asha shielded Fionn, as if her body could somehow protect him. But Kobi remained standing, facing the flames. For a second he thought of Hales. Then he thought of nothing.

"I'm sorry," he said to the others, then closed his eyes, feeling the inferno engulf him.

11

JUST AS THE SEARING heat from the flames became unbearable, the heat vanished, leaving his face tingling. He opened his eyes to see the fleet of Scorchers banking and flying back on a parallel path. Fire once again gushed over the ground below.

"Why did they stop?" asked Asha, staring at the departing drones in disbelief. Her face was covered in a sheen of sweat. The air shimmered. Smoke spiraled into the sky.

"I have no idea," said Kobi.

Asha tilted her head. "Wait." She crouched on the ground and poked a finger into the ashes. A tiny shrub sprang out from the dust, its delicate leaves reaching into the air.

Fionn waved his hand over the top, and it moved in time with him.

"It's Waste infected," rasped Yaeko, still lying on her front from when she had leaped to the ground, her lower back rising and falling as she drew deep breaths.

"Must have spread from the other side of the wall," said Kobi.

"I don't understand," said Yaeko, finally finding her feet. "Aren't the Scorchers supposed to wipe out plants like this?"

Kobi stared at the small writhing root. "Forest fires rejuvenate the ecosystem. Many plants and seeds survive fires belowground. I'm sure there are seeds everywhere under this desert waiting for the day the drones finally stop."

"Here," said Asha. She was bent over another small weed. Then, a few yards farther on, she found a cluster of more. They were camouflaged by a layer of sand. "All of these are Waste mutated." She pointed back the way they had come. "I can sense the plants going off that way, back toward the city."

Kobi checked his map and compass. "Yes, you're right. That direction will end up at the southern end of the mountains overlooking New Seattle. It's a direct route. We had to skirt east. That's why we didn't see any until now."

"I think you're right about CLAWS," said Asha. "They want the Waste to spread, just enough to keep people sick. They've programmed the Snatchers to leave a path of plants back to the city, through which Waste can spread."

"Kinda clever, really," said Yaeko. "Hey, look at this. The little weeds are growing."

Kobi looked down. The shoots were twisting up slowly. Cracks spread across the ground. Kobi could feel movement under his soles. He went still.

"What I don't get," said Asha, "is why these plants haven't grown any higher if the drones have stopped burning them."

"They have grown," said Kobi. "Just not upward. These are Chokers. Everybody, don't move."

The others froze. "What do we do?" whispered Yaeko.

"When I give the word, we run—all together. Ready . . ."

The earth exploded. Chokers like giant serpent bodies writhed muscularly in a blur of green and brown, towering into the sky. Dry earth cascaded down, buffeting Kobi's head and shoulders. He cowered under the deluge of soil, staring around for the others. He heard shouts and picked out the shapes and charged through the raining soil. He grabbed at the figures and pulled them away. They moved out of range of the falling earth but knew they weren't safe from the Chokers. He saw Asha and Yaeko next to him.

"Fionn!" said Asha. "Where is he?" She was already running back toward the Chokers, shouting Fionn's name.

Kobi turned after her. The Chokers reared up into the sky as high as a house, and the vines arched and flickered, almost like they were looking down at Kobi. *Why haven't they grabbed us?*

"Up here." The voice was strange but familiar. It sounded calm. Kobi looked up.

Fionn was silhouetted against the sky, caught in a tangle of Chokers. *Not caught*, thought Kobi. *He's being* carried.

"Fionn, you need to get down from there," said Asha.

"It's okay. They are friends," said Fionn.

Kobi realized it had been months since he'd heard the boy's

voice. It sounded hoarse and cracked, deeper than he remembered. Fionn had recovered the ability to speak while he was with Kobi and Asha in the Wastelands of Old Seattle, but he hadn't spoken since they'd arrived at the Sol base. It was no wonder, really, Kobi thought. Fionn was still scarred from a CLAWS lab experiment: they'd let loose a Waste-mutated bear in the hope that Fionn could use his powers to control the creature. The bear had killed a cluster of CLAWS scientists, ripping them apart before Fionn's eyes. Of course he hated being confined, hated being monitored by scientists at the Sol base. Now that he was free, back in the Wastelands, he seemed much more at ease. "We need to get over this wall, right?" said Fionn casually. A Choker wrapped around his waist and lowered him carefully toward the ground.

Kobi's mind was oddly transported back to something in his past, to sitting with his father in the base at Bill Gates High and watching the animated movie of *The Jungle Book*. Fionn seemed just like Mowgli being carried in the powerful trunk of the elephant. Kobi used to imagine he was Mowgli, a boy raised in the wild—it made him feel safe. But Kobi realized Fionn's connection to the Waste life went so much deeper than his own.

Fionn beckoned to Kobi and Asha and Yaeko. "Get behind me." They did as he asked. One of the Choker stalks crawled up the side of the concrete face like a giant snake, knocking large chunks of cement free as it went. After five minutes or so, the tip of the Choker was out of sight. After a while longer it must have reached the top, and the thick vine froze in place, twisted back and forth at a diagonal angle up the wall.

A smug smile spread across Fionn's face. "Time to climb." The Choker had clung to the concrete in the shape of something like a staircase, and Fionn began to clamber up a step at a time, using the spikelike thorns as grips when he needed.

More Jack and the Beanstalk than The Jungle Book, Kobi thought with a grin.

"I'm going up," said Yaeko. "Looks fun." She began to climb up after Fionn, making light work of it.

"I don't know if he can keep control of it," said Asha to Kobi. "What if it tries to throw us off?"

Kobi shrugged. "You saw Fionn with those rats. His powers are incredible. We have to trust him."

Asha watched Fionn and Yaeko, climbing up and laughing. "It's the first time he's spoken out loud in ages," she said.

"That has to be a good thing."

"I suppose," said Asha. "I sense that *anger* in him. Like it's making his powers stronger."

"He's not angry at you, Asha. He's angry at CLAWS, at what they did to him. We can't treat him like a little kid anymore."

Fionn waved down at them from twenty yards up, still grinning.

Kobi climbed, shifting his weight between his hands and feet as he reached for the next set of thorns. Kobi tried to block out the slight quivering he felt through his fingers. If the Choker shifted, they'd all be thrown to their deaths. What would Hales think if he could see him?

He climbed up after Fionn and Yaeko, fifty, a hundred yards into the sky. It felt good to be using his muscles again. The knowledge that he was only one missed grip away from falling to his death was invigorating. His mind felt focused, body alive.

It took almost an hour to reach the top. Kobi leaped up over the edge of the wall and onto the parapet. Yaeko and Fionn were sitting with their legs dangling over the far side, staring in silence at the endless Waste forest stretching as far as he could see.

"Wow," said Asha breathlessly as she rolled over the top of the wall.

There was a faint haze over the canopy; trees over five hundred feet tall. The largest were the cedars, golden auburn trunks with giant leaves like oversize satellite dishes glistening a dark emerald under the rays of sun. In the far distance Kobi could just make out the spindle shape of the Space Needle in the central district, wrapped up in clinging vines, the dark gray shapes of skyscrapers spread around it similarly clothed in green. Kobi felt a shiver as he spotted the drifting silhouettes of Snatchers flying out from the Space Needle or returning there to roost: that was where they were based, a CLAWS operating tower.

Kobi was suddenly aware of how exposed they were on top of the wall. "We need to get down into the canopy before we're spotted."

He took out his map and compass and fixed a bearing on the

Needle to pinpoint their exact position. Once he had it, it was straightforward to plot a course to Mercer Island. As long as they skirted the southern tip of Lake Sammamish, they'd be heading in the right direction.

"Looks like about twelve miles to reach the island," Kobi said. "We need to get some rest first though. Make camp somewhere." He tried to sound casual, but inside he was in turmoil. He'd never traveled so far in the Wastelands before. Any section of the journey might contain untold hazards. He looked around at the sweating faces of his companions as they turned to him, watching as he plotted the course. He knew they were relying on him. Their lives were in his hands. And Yaeko had never been out here. But having Fionn with them would surely make things safer. The boy didn't look worried. He looked eager.

"Follow what I say down there," Kobi said to Yaeko. "There's no time for games when everything is trying to kill you. I'll go through hand gestures and basic animal calls, but you have to do what I say immediately. I don't need to tell you to worry about Snatchers—but there are dangerous plants and animals too, and they're even more unpredictable."

"*They're not dangerous,*" said Fionn. *"Or unpredictable. Not if you're with me."*

"Okay, Fionn," said Asha. "But you can't expect to be able to control *everything* out there."

"Hales used to say that the second you stop respecting the environment it kills you," Kobi added. "That goes for you too,

Fionn. We only ever move one at a time, while the others cover the surroundings. And don't ever, ever go off on your own." Kobi paused. "I did that once in the Wastelands, the first time I came out here. It didn't go well." Asha caught his eye: she knew he was talking about meeting the mutated orca.

"Right, right, I got it. You're the boss," said Yaeko. "Believe me, I'm not going solo out here."

Asha opened her backpack and took out a syringe of Horizon.

"We need to take these," she said. "The concentration of Waste here is way higher than we're used to."

She handed a syringe to Yaeko, and they each injected it into their forearms. Fionn, though, hesitated. "*I don't need it,*" he said. "*I feel fine.*"

"Don't be stupid," said Asha. "Remember how sick you got last time we were here? You nearly died. You're not immune like Kobi." Reluctantly, Fionn administered the dose. Asha was right, Kobi thought. Fionn's state of mind didn't seem entirely healthy. It wasn't just the anger. It was like he believed in his connection to the Waste so much he was losing touch with his vulnerability to it. He was forgetting reality, and that could put both him, and the others, in danger.

After the medicine was packed away, Kobi approached Fionn, eager to keep him working as part of the team. "How about some more help?" He pointed to the nearest tree. "We need to get into the canopy. I think it could be a good place to make camp." Kobi patrolled the top of the wall. He found a ponderosa pine whose pinnacle was only a few-yard drop. Its needles were thick as his arm. He remembered collecting them to create pit-traps. They were strong. He leaped onto the branch. He helped the others down, but when it came to Fionn, the boy ignored his outstretched hand and bounded down. "Easy," he said with a grin.

They climbed carefully down to the lower canopy, slipping between thick branches and taking hold of leaves, which were easily strong enough to take their weight. Kobi looked along the enormous branch that they were now walking on. The forest was so thick here, the trees so colossal, it should be possible to stay off the ground completely. He checked his compass.

"Follow me."

As he cut a path through the branches, Kobi kept his eyes open. Perhaps it was being back in the Wastelands and the aura of the place dredging memories from Kobi's past, but Hales's voice felt louder than ever, guiding him with the old rules. Even when Kobi didn't want it to. *"Look and listen before you move. Watch for birds roosting amid the branches or when you're moving in open space. Move between points of cover."*

They started off in single file, Kobi up front hacking back any obstructing leaves or branches using a hard oak branch he'd sharpened with his knife into a makeshift machete. But soon Fionn was ranging ahead, swinging and hopping nimbly through the branches, completely at ease. Occasionally he would take a detour, disappearing for a couple of minutes at a time, before reappearing in front of them, seeming almost impatient.

Asha whispered urgently to him. "What did Kobi say about going off on your own?"

"He's making his own rules."

Kobi had been right; they didn't have to venture to the ground at all. The site of the long drop down, glimpsed between the branches, made his stomach swoop. They entered what had been the suburban outskirts of the city. Below, the remains of houses and other buildings were dimly visible though the greenery, completely overwhelmed by plants, with roofs caved in or walls collapsed under the weight of vines. Once they came across the shell of a church spire tipped on its side and carried up in a cradle of branches. The huge boulders scattered below seemed natural at first, but Kobi realized they were cars, left in an old parking lot, their rusted shells covered in moss.

A few shafts of sunlight penetrated the forest, but mostly it was gloomy under the shelter of the treetops and the vast leaves of ferns. Kobi kept them heading straight for the shores of Lake Washington, and as they traveled an anxiety began to gnaw at his gut. They were making okay progress, traveling through the Wastelands with Asha to sense dangers with her telepathy and Fionn to protect them from the Chokers, but the closer they got to the Park site, the more concentrated the Waste would be.

"I'm worried," said Asha. "Fionn's been gone ages."

Kobi rested against a branch, wiping the sweat from his brow. He hadn't noticed when Fionn last went off.

"He can't have gone that far," said Yaeko. As she drew up beside them, her skin rippled in shades of green. "I kind of think he's showing off."

Asha chewed her lip. "I can't sense him. There's so much Waste here. He's camouflaged."

She turned out to the foliage around them and raised her voice. "Fionn? Where are you?"

"Asha, quiet!" Kobi hissed, raising a hand. "We don't want to draw attention."

Just then the leaves in the branch above parted. Kobi gripped his stun baton. But it was Fionn's face that poked through.

"Fionn! You shouldn't keep running off," said Asha. "It's not safe."

Fionn looked at her curiously. "This is the safest we've ever been," he said. "Can't you see? We're free here."

Asha didn't appear to know what to say. "Fionn, I don't know what's gotten into you, but this place is dangerous. I know you can control it, but please, we have to stick together here. What if you injure yourself? You need Horizon." Fionn rolled his eyes and then held up his hand, drawing an enormous bluebottle from a nearby branch before shooing it away with a flick of his fingers.

The light through the canopy was dimming. Kobi saw that the thickest of the branches where they'd stopped had a deep gouge cut out of the trunk. Kobi inspected it. It was a giant termite hole. Judging from the moss that grew inside, he thought it must be old. It was just the right size for two of them to lie down in, side by side, and there was even a stubby branch to hang their packs on. "This is a good spot to sleep awhile. No predators will get to us in that hole." He decided not to mention what had made it.

"Sounds good to me," said Yaeko as Asha continued to glare at Fionn. "Maybe we just need to cool off."

Asha ignored them. "Just because you can't *see* the Waste, Fi, doesn't mean you're not breathing it in all the time. Every second we're here, we're dying."

Fionn pointed at Kobi. "Not if we have him. Kobi's blood can keep us alive. We can make more cleansers. We don't ever have to leave."

Kobi felt a chill. There was a manic look in Fionn's eye, like desperation. Kobi did understand how he must feel. This had been Kobi's home for thirteen years—it had been his whole world. Deep inside, part of him longed to turn things back to how they were. But at some point you had to break free of your past.

"You can't ignore the truth, Fionn. You can't just hide from it forever. That's what Hales tried to do with me."

Fionn clenched his jaw and shook his head.

"We can't stay here," Asha said. "We will never be safe. The Waste will always be trying to kill us. Fi, the Waste isn't good. It killed millions of people! It's still killing people."

Fionn's features took on a more determined look. "*People* have killed millions of people," he said. "People killed Rohan, and Mischik."

"We can stop CLAWS," said Asha, "when we find the cure. We can make people better."

Fionn looked around at the oversize growth in every direction. The voice that came through to Kobi's mind was sad. *"What if I don't want to be* better?*"* He lifted a hand, and the leaves around him bent inward as if answering his call. *"This is who I am."* Fionn looked at Kobi. *"You understand. We belong out here."*

Kobi said nothing for a moment. Then he remembered what Johanna had said about rage making Fionn's powers strong and helping him feel in control. Maybe Kobi could appeal to that rage. "I do know one thing. We're not going to let Melanie Garcia win. CLAWS is going to pay for what they did to us."

Fionn's expression hardened. He clenched his fists and nodded.

Asha continued, pleading, "Why are you being like this, Fionn?" Kobi could tell all the hurt and frustration she'd been bottling up was bursting to the surface. He put a hand on her shoulder, but she shrugged him off, stepping toward Fionn. "Your mutations . . . This is what CLAWS *made* you. It doesn't define you." She pointed around at them all. "We're all we've got. *People* make a home, not a place. Why can't you see that?"

"Asha, leave it," said Kobi. He thought clearly in his head, widening his eyes, trying to get her to read his thoughts. *"We need to make him feel strong, not like a victim."*

But if Asha read his thoughts, she didn't listen. "They infected you with Waste, Fionn, before you were even born. If you let your powers define you, they've won. Don't let them control your destiny."

Fionn turned on her, eyes flashing. His thoughts were projected accompanied by a wave of fury. *"Should I let you control my destiny instead?"*

"Fi, that's not what I meant!" she replied.

"Then stop telling me what to do!"

He turned and disappeared into the foliage. Kobi heard the shuffle of leaves as he scampered away. Asha shouted for him to come back.

"He'll come back," said Kobi. "If we all get lost, we'll only put ourselves in more danger. Give him some space for a while. He needs to figure out who he is without the Waste. I'm figuring out the same thing."

"We all are," said Asha quietly, sitting down on a large knot bulging out from the tree branch.

Kobi didn't want to admit it to Asha, but he *was* worried about Fionn; he didn't have a compass or a map. Kobi thought back to his first training session in the Wastelands. *"Never run off again. Got it?"*

And, thinking selfishly, Kobi knew that they needed Fionn. Without him, without his ability to control Waste organisms, they might not make it to Mercer Island.

They made camp, laying out blankets inside the termite hole. Yaeko chatted on awkwardly, mostly complaining about the hardness of the tree branch, about getting eaten alive by mosquitoes—literally. But Kobi knew in her own way she was trying to make Asha feel better. Yaeko handed out some flatbread; supplies were almost out. They'd need to start scavenging tomorrow.

"I'll take first watch," said Asha. She took the stun baton from Kobi. "Don't think I could sleep anyway while Fionn's missing."

Kobi found some strong-smelling flowers in a nearby tree that would mask their scent and repel insects. They couldn't afford a fire: the smoke and heat signatures might attract Snatchers. At least the tightly knotted branches of the oak kept them protected, and the nearby fir trees were dotted with giant cones that had mutated protective spikes, which would also deter predators.

Kobi crawled into the hollow alongside Yaeko. "Almost makes me miss the dorms at Sol," she said, wriggling to get comfortable. Soon she was snoring softly. Kobi became aware of another sound: the occasional gentle sob or sniff. He looked over at Asha. He couldn't imagine the strong, determined girl crying; the sight of it shocked him. He climbed back out of the hole and sat opposite her silently. He waited for her to speak when she was ready.

"I know you think the same thing as Fionn," she said eventually, her voice firm as she wiped away the tears. "That I'm too controlling: the ways I read your mind and boss you around."

Kobi began to protest, but Asha continued. "You know, the problem with being able to read people's thoughts is that you see things they don't. You want to help them, but it only pushes them away. It's frustrating." She was quiet a few more seconds, and her eyes were glassy. "You know, I never told you before. It was me who convinced Fionn to help CLAWS with the experiment with the bear. He was scared, but I told him it would be okay. I was doing it for Melanie. She wanted it so badly that I did too, just to make her happy. "

"It's not your fault," Kobi said.

"I should have protected him, but I didn't. I betrayed his trust." She peered into the darkness among the branches. "Just like with you. When I called in the Snatchers at the lab."

Kobi was taken aback for a moment. "You thought you were making the right decision."

"Everyone *thinks* they're doing the right thing," said Asha.

Kobi had never seen her feeling so low before. "That's not true," he said. "I bet Melanie Garcia doesn't."

Wordlessly, Asha reached inside her jacket and pulled out a small folded piece of paper or card. Kobi frowned at it, and as she opened it, his heart thudded. It was a photo. Even before she turned it for him to see fully, he recognized what it showed. He couldn't believe it. He thought he'd never see it again. It was a photo of him and Hales taken on a Polaroid camera about two years ago while they were still at Bill Gates. They stood side by side, arms around each other. Kobi felt a well of emotion overcome him.

"How did you get that?" he asked, voice quiet.

"I took it," she said. "From the school where you lived with Hales, when you took me, Fionn, and Niki back there. It was just in case we got separated, so I could prove to CLAWS we'd found you. I . . . stole it, and then, afterward at Sol, I wanted to give it to you, but I thought it would be better if you forgot about Hales. I thought you'd be angry too."

For a moment he felt a prickle of anger, then he sighed. "I understand," he said, and took it carefully. "Thank you for keeping it for me."

She wiped her eyes. "No problem. He loved you, you know. Despite the lies. It doesn't stop him from being your dad."

Kobi felt his own eyes go moist, blurring the faces of the images of Hales and himself grinning, arm in arm. Hales's words echoed through the night, from when he'd just rescued Kobi from the orca.

"I thought I'd lost you. I thought I lost you, son."

"I'm going to sleep," said Kobi, feeling a little embarrassed at all the emotions. "Wake me up in a few hours and I'll take over. And don't worry. Fionn will come back."

She smiled at him. "Sure."

Kobi joined Yaeko in the termite hole, trying to get comfortable. The chorus of the forest grew louder in the evening: the spine-chilling howls of wolves in the distance, the flap of giant bird wings—ravens, Kobi guessed from the rhythm of the wing beats—and the hum of giant lethal insects. He drifted through memories that rose like bubbles from the depths of his mind, thoughts he hadn't dwelled on since he'd first left the city. Mostly they were small things: the smell of the gym back at the school, the simple meals he and Hales had enjoyed by candlelight, the old DVDs they'd watched on the battered TV hooked up to the solar generator. . . . The flashes of the past soothed him, made him feel safe.

But the last words he thought of before sleep overtook him were Asha's.

People *make a home, not a place.*

12

KOBI WOKE, INSTANTLY ALERT. He'd slept too long. Dusk was coming. He climbed from the termite hole, leaving Yaeko snoring softly, a strand of drool hanging from the corner of her mouth. Asha had fallen asleep on her watch. She was leaning back against the bulbous tree knot, head lolling and eyes closed. Fionn's head rested on her lap, pillowed with a thick, waxy oak leaf. Kobi felt a deep relief at seeing Fionn safe. For a while he watched them as the younger boy's head rose and fell with Asha's slow, peaceful breathing.

Taking care to keep quiet, Kobi lifted himself higher into the web of thick, twisting branches, using the large twigs as hand-holds, and before long he had picked his way twenty feet higher, up into the sparser upper canopy. Straddling a few interconnected branches and supporting his shoulder against another, he took out the map of Old Seattle from his pocket. Trying not to think about the seemingly endless drop below, he scanned the map, comparing it to a distant stretch of water he could see through the branches, and beyond that, the gray towers of central Seattle. Kobi estimated his position to be somewhere on the outskirts of the city, close to the southern part of the area once called Bellevue, which meant it was only a mile or so until they'd reach the shores of Lake Washington—the body of water he could see ahead, in the middle of which lay Mercer Island. The trees blocked his view of the nearer part of the lake. There was a bridge marked on the map, linking Bellevue with Mercer Island. Kobi had crossed it out with a pencil, replicating his dad's map: all the bridges from Mercer Island had been blown up in the days after the disastrous launch of GAIA as the military tried to contain the Waste. They'd have to get across some other way.

"Stay away from the water, Kobi, at all costs!"

"This time we don't have much choice, Dad," said Kobi. *Dad.* Kobi realized he'd called Hales that again. Whether the word had come automatically because Kobi was back in Old Seattle, where he had lived with Hales as father and son, or if there was some deeper feeling that had been stirred inside him by the photo Asha had given him, Kobi couldn't work out.

Climbing back down, he glanced across at Fionn. On their last trip to the Wastelands, Fionn had nearly died twice, his body overwhelmed by Waste, shutting down. They had Horizon now, but the closer they got to Mercer Island, the more concentrated the Waste. Perhaps Horizon would hold the Waste back; perhaps it wouldn't. He remembered the last drone message sent by Jonathan Hales.

"It's going to be difficult to get there, impossible for me—for everyone—but there is one person who can do it. Kobi!"

Kobi would much rather that others could come with him, and he'd have a hard time persuading Fionn he couldn't come.

Kobi coughed loudly, and Fionn and Asha stirred. They stretched, looking around confused.

Their features were drawn, eyes rimmed with red, and they got to their feet stiffly. "I feel so tired," said Asha.

"It's the Waste," said Kobi. "We're getting closer to Mercer Island, where the contamination is stronger. You both need to take some more cleansers. So does Yaeko." He called over to the termite hole, softly. "Yaeko!"

The girl peered out, hair falling in a mess over her face. "What!" Her throat sounded dry, and she coughed. "I don't feel good."

Kobi watched as Asha handed her a syringe, and the others all took their cleansers. He wondered how long the dosage would last. The Waste in their blood would retreat for a few hours, but out here, in the heart of the Wastelands, it wouldn't be long before it came back even stronger.

"When we get to the lake, I'll go on alone." He tried to keep his voice firm, but the truth was the thought filled him with dread. "You guys are too sick. Hales said in his message that I had to go out there—that only I could survive."

Asha shook her head. Yaeko was nodding hers. "What?" said

Yaeko, holding up her hands as Asha frowned at her. "Hales knew his stuff! Kobi thinks he needs to go out on his own, and I think he's right. We can't survive the epicenter of the Waste."

"Hales didn't know about us," said Fionn.

Kobi nodded. It was true. He could see there was no point arguing. "We'll monitor your condition," he said. "But remember that we'll need to up your dosage of Horizon and we don't want to run out later on."

They headed out. The trees became sparser, and Kobi noticed that several seemed to be dying, their branches drooping or their trunks twisted or split open, bare of leaves. One span that looked sturdy enough must have been rotten because it cracked under Asha's feet and almost sent her falling to the forest floor. They decided to descend to ground level. They found a conifer with branches growing close together and long solid spindles that could be used like ladder rungs. Yaeko went first, scuttling down and swinging and leaping between them with a smug grin on her face. She pointed out routes and gave them advice on how to get lower. It wasn't always appreciated.

"Reach your left foot, Asha. Come on. A little more."

"A little more and I'll fall."

"You've just got to trust me."

"Yeah, that's the problem!"

As they reached the lowest main branch forking off from the trunk, Kobi made everyone wait, hidden, as he listened and watched for any signs of movement. *"Patience is your greatest protection, Kobi."* He gave a signal and they hopped down one by one, keeping low in a field of patchy, dry gorse. There was a cluster of spotty brown mushrooms ahead, each as big as a pitcher's mound, but they were falling apart and gave off a putrid stench. The trees were sparse and leafless, their bark moldy and diseased.

"I don't get it," Asha said. "The Waste's stronger than ever here. But things are dying."

"Maybe it's *too* much Waste," said Kobi. "At these levels it must even be toxic to plants and animals."

Yaeko winced and rubbed her eyes. "Tell me about it," she said. "I've got the worst headache, and my stomach feels like it's going to heave up my lunch. If you can call a tiny piece of flatbread lunch. Those mushrooms smell gross."

Kobi felt a tingle of dread. "Maybe you guys should wait here—really, I can go on alone."

"No way," said Fionn, his expression fierce.

"We told you. We're in this together," said Asha. Her brown skin shone with an unhealthy sheen of sweat.

"Yeah, just try and stop us," said Yaeko, unconvincingly. Her voice cracked into a wheeze. "Actually, don't."

Kobi scanned the terrain. "We'll be on more open ground from now on. Keep your eyes peeled for trouble. You sense anything, Asha?"

"Only the trees." She scratched her head. "They sound almost . . . in pain. The Waste, it feels different here. Like it's one thing. I can't hear the plants and animals anymore, just . . . the

Waste itself, drowning everything else out."

Kobi experienced a feeling of dread that he realized now had been growing since they had had begun to get close to the diseased landscape—a kind of panicky fear spreading at the back of his mind—and he wondered if it was just the quiet, or if it was something else. Something from outside himself. He cut off his thoughts before they could unsettle him too much. "Okay, let's go. I move first. Wait for my signal."

They scurried one by one from the shade of one tree to another, but soon the earth became muddy and dark and sucked at their shoes, and the trees died away to broken stumps as big as jeeps.

They reached a single large building, with slithering vines moving in all the broken windows. Fionn grinned and held up his hand, and the vines twisted up into the air, waving back. Asha glanced at him uneasily.

Kobi saw a sign and could just make out a few letters in flaking paint: "SOUTH BELLEVUE GOLF COURSE." The greens and fairways were brown and sparse.

"I don't like this place," Asha said.

"Me neither," said Kobi.

They moved more quickly and reached higher ground on the far side of the course. Beneath them a freeway snaked past, choked with the wrecks of cars and collapsed in places where landslides had torn down the hillside. Beyond that was a vast expanse of dark water filled with low-lying mist. It looked more like a swamp than a lake, and fear stole over Kobi's heart at the sight, an instinctive stab that took him right back to the orca.

He took a long breath and checked the map. Mercer Island was within sight from the shore, but the flat water seemed to him to stretch forever. In his memory Hales stood in front of him, speaking urgently.

"Never go near the water, Kobi, under any circumstances. There are things in there. Terrible things. Always stick to dry land."

Something pushed him from behind. He turned to protest, but it was Asha, with her finger over her lips. She pointed to the sky. A moment later Kobi heard it: a mechanical buzzing sound.

Snatcher!

Yaeko beckoned them toward a tree that had fallen nearby, exposing a tangled nest of roots that formed a sort of shelter. They scrambled toward it, cramming together. Through the twisted roots, Kobi saw a shape drifting overhead, at a height of maybe a hundred feet. It wasn't a Snatcher. It was smaller, a simple disc shape with an array of reflective panels underneath. It doubled back. Kobi squinted at the drone. He had never seen anything like it before. It had no weapons that he could make out, but that didn't mean it couldn't summon dozens of Snatchers in an instant.

He could hear the breathing of the others around him. Yaeko gave a slight cough, and the drone juddered in the sky, dropping lower. Yaeko slammed her hand over her mouth, and Kobi's heart rattled. After a second, the drone moved off again. They waited a good five minutes before emerging from their hiding place. The sky was clear once more.

"Sorry," said Yaeko. "My cough is back."

"*We know,*" came Fionn's voice in Kobi's head.

"Hey!" said Yaeko. She bent over. "I think I need more cleansers."

"We need to ration them," said Asha. "Sorry."

Yaeko grumbled as Kobi set off ahead in a low crouch. Occasionally he saw scurrying ripples of insects and rodents. He kept his stun baton ready.

They walked down the slope toward the lake's edge. A row of old wooden houses, mostly collapsed, lined the shore. Their timbers were brown and rotting. Mist hung over the water ahead, seeping up over the swampy bank. They had to pick their way carefully. Everything felt dead, with a rotten stench filling the air. They didn't talk. Yaeko's muffled coughing and the squelch of their footsteps were the only sounds, eerily hollow under the cushioning fog.

"Never trust the silence, Kobi. It means something is out there. The Wastelands sense danger before you do."

Kobi edged closer to the lake's lapping edge. He imagined a dark shape rising up from the depths. The others held back. Unlike the water in Elliott Bay where Kobi had been attacked by the orca, here it was black and still, completely covered in a layer of algae that looked like thick, lumpy tar. Half-sunken boats jutted from the shallows.

Whether Fionn meant to project it or not, Kobi sensed his fear: being back in the Wastelands for the first time, he was scared.

There was Waste here but nothing life-giving.

"I don't see a way across," said Yaeko. "What's the plan, Caveman?"

Kobi glanced up and down the shore, and spotted what he was looking for. At the back of one of the derelict houses was a trailer covered in an old tarp. He walked over and cut through the bindings with his makeshift machete. Underneath was a ten-foot motorboat—in the filth of their surroundings it gleamed like something from another world.

"Help me get it to the water," he said.

They lifted one end of the trailer together and rolled it down toward the water's edge, then let the boat slide on its rollers into the water with less of a splash than a sickly squelch. It sent a thick ripple out into the lake. Kobi waited for it to settle.

"Do you know how to get it started?" asked Asha.

"It won't," said Kobi. "Any gas in the tank must have gone bad years ago."

You can do this. Treading cautiously, but trying to look unafraid, he waded into the shallows, pausing every few steps to scan for movement. The water was clammy around his ankles. He climbed into the boat and opened one of the side compartments beneath the seats. His senses screamed at him to get out of the water. The first compartment contained cushions, but the one opposite had two oars.

Asha, still standing on the shore, had her hands on the stern.

"Kobi," she said, jutting her chin toward the water. "I can feel something. Out there."

He paused. "What?"

"I don't know."

"An animal?"

"Maybe." She frowned as if trying to order her own thoughts. "It's like . . . It wants us to come to it."

Kobi swallowed. The truth was, Kobi could sense something too even though he had no telepathic powers. The strange panicky terror. It went through his whole body, tingling his skin, making his heartbeat explode in fits of palpitations he couldn't stop, no matter how much he tried to calm himself.

"I can go on alone," he said again. "You've taken me this far." The words wavered at the thought of being on his own: suddenly it seemed so much worse. *I have to. We have no choice.*

Asha shook her head. "We have more Horizon. We can go with you." Fionn nodded quickly.

"You're all sick," he said. "It's only going to get worse."

"He's kinda right," said Yaeko. She held up her hands. "Just saying." She coughed into one hand, louder than before. "That wasn't fake."

Fionn was already climbing into the boat. *"Kobi needs us."*

"I'm going too," said Asha, boarding. "You can stay here, Yaeko, but you'll be on your own."

Yaeko hugged herself. "Well, that sounds great." She put her hands on the edge of the boat and swung a leg over. "Guess I'm coming."

"If we run into trouble, we can turn back," said Kobi. He surveyed the dead water. *As long as whatever's out there lets us.*

He took one oar, and Asha the second. They pushed off. Dipping the oars into the thick scum, they paddled, slow and steady, across the water. Kobi kept his eyes on the surface, looking for any sign of movement. Asha was staring out ahead, through the pall of slithering mist. Kobi had the odd, illogical impression that they were rowing toward nothingness or an abyss of some sort, a dark emptiness that expanded and contracted like some massive, living, malevolent *thing*. His eyes struggled to focus on any landmark—it made him dizzy and left him blinking. Each time he dipped the paddle into the water, it was swallowed by blackness. Yaeko rubbed her temples, and Kobi realized he had a headache too. Was the Waste making him ill? How was that possible? *I'm supposed to be immune.*

The mist thickened, closing over them and blocking off any view of the shore from which they'd set out. There was no clear sight on the island ahead either, and for a few seconds Kobi felt lost, directionless, and his heart beat faster. Then, just as the claustrophobia reached an unbearable pitch and he was thinking about turning back, the mist opened up again, delivering a glimpse of their destination. Just a dark, shallow, featureless landmass. He paddled more urgently. Above the swish of his oar in the water, he heard one of the others whisper but couldn't make out the words.

"What?" he asked.

"Huh?" said Asha.

The whispering sound started again, but this time it came from somewhere to their left.

"I heard it too," said Yaeko quietly. "A voice. I don't like this."

They looked at one another as the hushed words—or maybe they weren't words, more a sigh—drifted across the lake.

"Hello?" called Asha. "Who's there?"

But there was no reply.

"I feel sick," said Yaeko. Kobi struggled to focus on her, his vision swimming.

"I feel weird too," said Asha.

Fionn suddenly retched, grabbing the side of the boat and throwing up over the side. Asha dropped her oar and went to him. "We need another dose of Horizon," she said grimly.

The sight of Fionn made Kobi's own stomach lurch. Yaeko dished out more syringes, and they injected themselves. He thought of his conversation with Johanna about his powers, how he had believed he had a connection with the Waste, like he needed it. *Shouldn't the Waste be making me stronger?* Kobi wondered if *he* should take the Horizon. *Maybe I was wrong. Is the Waste so strong here, it's getting to me too? Or is this something else . . . ? A warning?* But Kobi felt himself pulled onward, like the crippling weight affecting him was also some kind of magnetic pull. He found his thoughts were slow and confused. *I need to go on. I need to go on.*

Kobi wasn't sure how long they'd been rowing. Had it been ten minutes or an hour? How much farther could it be? "We should be close," he said, and his voice sounded odd in his ears. He was half trying to convince himself. He could barely talk from panic. Every second was a battle with the creeping, gnawing waves of fear that rippled down his shoulder blades, as if the waves were a physical force originating from somewhere outside him. Calling. Warning. But somehow intoxicating.

Yaeko moaned. "We have to turn back," she said. "My head's pounding. I feel really sick."

Kobi heard himself agree, but he only rowed harder. Something was drawing him toward the island. He dipped the oar again and dragged them closer.

"Kobi," said Asha. "I think she's right. There's something in the air. I think it's this mist."

Her voice sounded distant, and though Kobi heard her words, they didn't make sense to him, as if they were in another language. There was another voice speaking to him, and it urged him to come to the island. It welcomed him.

"Kobi?" Fionn, his voice clearer, spoke his name. *"Kobi, what's wrong?"*

Kobi turned to see all three of them looking in his direction. Yaeko could barely hold herself upright, and Asha's lips were moving, but no sounds were coming out.

"I've got to keep going," he said. He dipped the oar again.

"No," said Fionn. *"I was wrong, Kobi! Listen. We can't make it*

out here! Take us back." A pause. *"He's not listening. We've got to stop him."*

He's talking about me!

Asha reached for him and took hold of the paddle, but Kobi ripped it free. The boat rocked as he fell down beside the wheel. The other three were looking at him, afraid. What was wrong with them?

Asha grabbed the paddle again, as did Fionn. *"Give it to us!"* said Fionn. *"You're not thinking straight."*

But the island was calling. And it was close. Kobi looked at his companions, then went to the edge of the boat.

"What are you doing?" said Asha.

I have to go to it. I have to.

He heard Asha call out his name as he jumped over the side, plunging into the black, rotting abyss. The cold shock of the water left him reeling, and sudden darkness closed over him. Splashing to the surface, he twisted, looking for the boat, but it was gone. The mist kept him from seeing anything. It curled around him, forming animal-like shapes or the tendrils of Chokers. They reached into his mouth, ears, down his throat. Somewhere Asha was calling his voice, shrill and terrified. The panic sharpened his senses. Why had he jumped? It was crazy. Black algae weighed down his arms, filled his nostrils with its rancid stench. Which way was the boat? He could still hear Asha but not clearly. There was another presence, a wordless voice—the dread itself entering his head, pulling him, urging him on.

I have to go to the voice, thought Kobi. Lifting his arms through the heavy algae, his heart feeling like it wanted to burst from his chest, Kobi swam, trying to keep the water from sloshing into his mouth. He saw the island dimly, a smudge of gray rising out of the water, and adjusted his course. He could make it. Part of him worried about the others, but that part was drowned out by his own instinct for survival, by the magnetic fear calling to him.

The Waste. That's what it is. The Waste itself. It knows me. It remembers me.

The water swelled not far ahead, a large wave, rippling out like something was just beneath the surface. Terror screamed in his ears. Kobi glided to a stop, barely daring to kick out and disturb the black lake around him. Something broke the surface. His heart seemed to stop for a moment, his entire rib cage clenching over it like a fist. It was a tall black fin, cutting like a gleaming knife. And he knew, suddenly, where he was. Back in the past. Back in the water. Kobi was just nine years old again, lost, alone. And it was coming for him.

"Dad!" he called out. "I need you! Help me."

The creature from the deep had come to take him. The fin sliced toward Kobi, slipping beneath the surface as it headed in his direction. All Kobi could do was tread water, waiting, his legs dangling and exposed. The predator could snatch him under at any moment. A gap in the mist opened up, and the island shore was close—maybe thirty yards away. He might not get another chance.

He screamed and thrashed, windmilling his arms, kicking his legs, heaving a wake through the clogging algae.

The voice that had called to him was gone, replaced with a howling, screeching echo from the water itself. The orca's call, like a siren. Others answered, and on his right Kobi saw two more fins slicing up. *A pod. They're everywhere.*

They were converging toward him at a leisurely pace, playing with him.

Only twenty yards to shore, but there was no chance he could make it. He spotted another swell to his left; there were more. A body rose above the waterline, a hulking mass of scarred black flesh. It turned quite suddenly, striking out toward him. Kobi stopped swimming, transfixed, staring at his own death. Kobi saw a head half above the water. Gleaming yellow eyes. A pink-gummed mouth more elongated than a natural orca's—almost like a crocodile's—and gaping yards wide, lined with hundreds of teeth bigger than him. A stink of rottenness. Kobi threw his arms in front of his face, bracing for the massive jaws to crush his body.

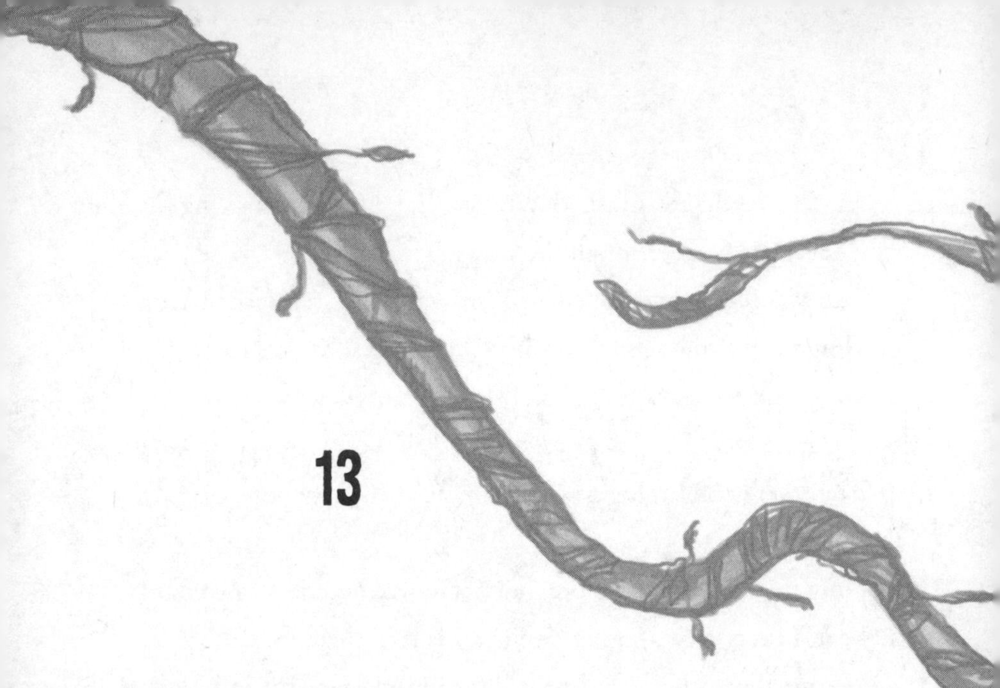

13

THEY NEVER CAME. AS Kobi lowered his arms, the killer whale was gone, and the water was still. Completely still. A shiver wracked his limbs. There were no fins. No sounds. No danger.

I imagined all of it.

The realization cleared his mind a little. Slowly, the screeching panic left him, leaving only the same dull fear as before, spreading into his mind and clouding his thoughts.

Was it testing me? Whatever is calling me?

He was able to swim again, the last few yards, toward the shore. Soon he could put down his feet into the sludge of the lake bed. He dragged himself onto swampy land, rolled over onto his back. For a moment he lay there. The headache was gone, his mind clear.

I made it, but what about the others?

He stood up, feet sinking to ankle depth in the mud. "Asha?" he called. "Fionn?

No one replied. He called again, and again, until his voice was hoarse. He told himself they'd be okay. Prayed they didn't come any nearer. If they'd returned to the mainland, they might be all right. *If they're hurt, it's my fault. I kept rowing. Why? Why did I do it?*

The guilt fell away. All he felt was the presence of the island, dark and foreboding, at his back.

"I'm alone," he whispered into the wind, which was humid, rippling his damp clothes as if searching him. "You were right, Dad. I had to come here by myself."

He trudged up the shoreline, sinking with each stride as the ground sucked at his feet. The mist here was just as thick, and each time he stepped, more of it seemed to rise from the mud. Every so often, he would trip on a root—they threaded through the mud, pale as bones, only to emerge in stubby, twisted trees that reached inland with skeletal branches as if blasted by an invisible wind.

The stunted forest thickened, with trees intertwined or sprouting up alone only for their branches to join another trunk high above, giving the impression that the whole forest was one giant entangled morass. In some places, from the corner of his eye, Kobi thought he even saw roots twitch or jerk, tightening their grip on the earth or folding over one another in a sinister embrace. He stepped with care, trying to stay clear, and stranger sights appeared through the mist. Here, farther from the water, the trees weren't completely dead. Some had leaves, rustling in a breeze he couldn't feel. Before his eyes the leaves swelled on their stems before blackening and falling to the ground. More replaced them, growing, then wilting as he watched. There were flowers too, flashes of color, growing from vines that tangled around the branches. Their petals trembled, then curled over and floated to the swampland, where they were swallowed. Fungi swelled, then burst, showing the fibers of their innards before crumbling to dust.

As he pushed deeper, among the rapid cycles of nature, the voices came again. Whispers at first, which came from the trees. He couldn't make out the words, but they were at once comforting and exhilarating, filling his chest with a feeling of belonging. *You belong here. This place is yours. Stay with us. Be with us.* He breathed deeply, letting the Waste fill his lungs, almost sensing it in his blood pumping to every part of him. He'd never felt more alive. Ahead a strange round ball of leafy material swelled like a tumor from the slimy earth. Kobi stared at it. Suddenly it exploded, sending a cloud of spores into the air in a violent gust. Kobi held up a hand, but the spores covered his face, entering his nose and mouth, and for a second his vision swam with strange colors, and the voice screamed in his ear.

You're with us now.

His foot snagged, and he tried to pull it up, but it was held fast. Looking down, he saw a root had fully encircled his ankle. As he tugged again, it slithered farther around his lower leg, doubling the loop.

You're with us now, Kobi.

"No!" he said. He kicked at the root, then pulled out the Swiss army knife from his buttoned pocket and hacked as close to his foot as he dared, and the blade bit into the white fibrous flesh of the root. It recoiled, but then it tightened and suddenly jerked his foot into the ground, so he sank to his knee. Kobi flailed for balance, crashed down on the other knee as a second white tendril climbed up to his waist. He tried to swing the knife, but something had his wrist too. As it squeezed, he dropped the blade. The power of the white roots was unyielding and astonishing, dragging his arm toward the ground.

Don't fight us. Let us take you.

The voice was calm, but the sensation was anything but. The ground had turned more liquid, and he sank farther, up to his chest.

"Help!" he yelled though he knew no one could hear. "Help me!"

More tendrils of pale wood, knotty and covered in dirt, climbed his torso, encircled his neck. The pressure, when it came, cut off his air at once. He still had one arm free, and he slid a finger between the root and his skin. He managed to pry the root away long enough to draw a breath, but another snaking root took that hand too.

"Help!" he choked as the water bubbled up around his neck. More delicate roots were sprouting, exploring his face like fingers, brushing his eyes. He wanted to scream, but his mouth was going under.

Just as he swallowed a clot of choking mud, a shape appeared through the mist—a human shape and a point of flickering orange light.

"Dad!" Kobi called, a shard of hope penetrating through the confusion clouding his mind. "I'm over here. Pull me out!"

But as the figure approached, Kobi saw it wore a biohazard suit. His whole body jerked with horror.

CLAWS.

They'd found him. He scrambled one last time but knowing he could never get free. The CLAWS agent lifted something metallic. Gun-shaped. A jet of flame lit up the air, directed right toward him.

He woke screaming, throwing up his arms. Everything was too bright, and he had to clamp his eyes closed. His mouth felt gritty. But slowly he managed to squint into the light.

And nothing made sense.

He was lying in a comfortable single bed with metal posts, on linen as white as fresh snow. The room around him was a child's bedroom, with shelves of picture books and wooden models of trains and cars. On a shelf, a one-eyed teddy bear sat slumped at an angle. Beside the bed on a small table, there was an old-fashioned alarm clock and a family photograph. A man and a woman holding a baby on a beach somewhere and a little boy of about seven kicking sand.

A breeze tickled the thin curtains. The smells of flowers and fresh-cut grass reached Kobi's nose.

It must be a dream, he thought, *or another hallucination.*

At least it was a nice one.

He pushed the blanket off his legs and climbed out of bed. He was wearing sweatpants and a crisp blue T-shirt, too big for him. "Seattle Seahawks," Kobi muttered, peering down at the logo of the bird.

Just beneath his elbow, a clean bandage was neatly fastened, but it didn't hurt. His bare feet met worn wooden floorboards. It all felt so real, and he realized the horrible taste in his mouth was the earth that had almost suffocated him back on the island. The memory of the figure in the biohazard suit returned. Or had that all been part of the hallucination too?

His ankle was sore, and the skin was covered in faint red welts where the roots had gripped him. So that had been real, at least. If it hadn't healed yet, it couldn't have been long ago. How had he gotten here so quickly? And where were his friends?

CLAWS must have taken me here, he realized, looking around. *Wherever* here *is. And why? Why wouldn't they just kill me? Is this all some trick to make me feel comfortable, to get information out of me?*

Kobi could finally think clearly. His head felt light. The fogginess had vanished, and the terror constricting his chest had lifted, leaving a lightness. *I must have been taken away from the island. How long have I been out?*

At the window, he pulled back the curtain and looked out

onto a large yard below. A beautiful lawn, showered by sprinklers, surrounded by beds of flowers and bushes, with three sprawling trees in the center—oaks, he thought. But there was no Waste here—all the plant life below was healthy. Normal. A greenhouse at one side reflected the sun. Through a gate to one side, on a gravel patch, he could see the front end of a 4x4 vehicle. Kobi was stumped; he could find nothing, no way to explain what he was seeing. There was something oddly familiar about the yard. He recognized aspects of it—the greenhouse and the plant beds and the massive towering hedges at the back—like he'd been here before, and he considered again if he was still dreaming or hallucinating. That might explain the déjà vu.

He crossed the room. His clothes were hanging over a rail, but they'd been washed and were damp to the touch. Over the back of a chair was a robe. A few sizes too big, but he put it on anyway. He went to the bedroom door. It opened with a creak onto a wide second-floor landing lined with more doors and paneled with wood. The place didn't look anything like Healhome. There were huge gilt-framed paintings on the wall. A strip of thick carpet ran over the floorboards to a stairway. Kobi smelled something—food—that made his stomach growl, drifting up from the bottom of the stairs.

"Hello?" he called, and his voice seemed to drift away. No one answered.

He resisted trying any of the other doors and descended the

stairway, footsteps creaking. He'd never been in a place so grand, so old—and one that wasn't riddled with Waste-infected plants. He almost felt like he was disturbing it, like the whole place was fragile. He could imagine a butler appearing from around a corner.

Light streamed through the front windows into an entrance hallway. A grandfather clock ticktocked gently. Treading lightly, Kobi peered through a door into an ornate dining room filled with silver ornaments on a table and shelves, and at one end was a large fireplace stacked with wooden logs. *It's almost something out of a fairy tale*, thought Kobi—but those stories were always dark, violent tales. The next room was a living room with a large piano and several plush leather couches.

Kobi thought about ripping open the large mahogany door in the spacious entrance hall and fleeing. But some instinct told him not to—or maybe it was just the curiosity of exploring. He moved into the kitchen and picked up a small knife. *Still, can't hurt to be prepared.* He padded lightly to a porch leading to a golden rectangle of light: the doorway looked like it framed another idealized painting of a landscape. Except it was real.

Kobi stepped out into the luscious yard. Again he was struck by a sense of familiarity. *When would I have been here before?* He walked down the gravel path past the 4x4, which looked clean and recently hosed down. The entire side of the house was surrounded by the same enormous hedge that obscured the view from the bedroom window.

Lying over a garden chair was a biohazard suit—the same one, he thought, that whoever rescued him had been wearing. He saw movement through the glass panels of the greenhouse. Kobi froze, then ducked behind the patio table, watching. The man inside, with his back to Kobi, was down on one knee among the plants. He wore a brown wool sweater. Kobi caught a flash of white hair. A sudden, illogical thought sent a jolt through his heart. *Hales? Dad? Was it actually him that saved me?*

"Dad . . . ," he called, approaching.

The man paused, stood stiffly, then turned around. It wasn't Hales. He was considerably taller or at least would have been if age hadn't bent him over. He had a long, lined face and large ears partially obscured by shaggy white hair that fell to an equally bedraggled beard. His eyes were pale green, watery, behind circular, wire-rimmed spectacles. One of his hands clutched the head of his walking stick, the joints knotted and painful looking. The other hand held a basket of ripe tomatoes.

"Hendrix mentioned you'd woken up," he said. His voice was soft. "How are you feeling?"

"Who are you?" Kobi asked. He had no idea who Hendrix was. Perhaps there *was* a butler somewhere. "Where are we? What happened?"

"That's a lot of questions," said the man. He took a step toward Kobi and paused. "I'll need that knife, by the way. These tomatoes won't cut themselves."

Kobi felt a little foolish, brandishing the blade, but he wasn't ready to give it up. "Answer me!" he said.

The man smiled, quite infuriatingly. "Very well. In answer to the first question: I'm Dr. Alan Apana. Second, we're at my house. And third: what happened? Well, that's rather a long story, and I imagine you're hungry. Will you join me for some lunch?"

14

HE WALKED PAST KOBI, ignoring the knife still clutched in his hand, and began to hobble toward the house. Kobi's legs felt unsteady, as if perhaps the ground itself was shifting.

Alan Apana. The founder of GrowCycle. The man who launched GAIA.

The man who thought he was god and destroyed the world, killing millions.

Surely he's dead. . . . That's what everyone thought.

Kobi watched the elderly white-haired man, very much alive, disappear through the back door.

He followed. Apana washed the tomatoes in the sink.

"You rescued me," Kobi said.

"My drone saw you and your friends approaching. You're lucky. Normally I don't venture into the Waste-infected areas unless I really have to. Cutting that root away from your limb was pretty difficult, I can tell you. Had to use my chainsaw. Steady hand, Alan, steady hand! Don't take off his arm! But as soon as I got one root away, another of the damned things grabbed you. They seemed to like the taste of you. Once you were dead, the Waste bacteria would have decayed your corpse in minutes. Your molecules would have become part of the clonal organism. When I finally got you in the jeep, you weren't in a good way. I thought you might not make it. The Waste-spore poisoning is potent."

Kobi felt sick, and Apana's words did nothing to rid him of the nausea and confusion swimming inside his skull. "But . . . how did you get me out of the Wastelands?" Kobi asked. "Did you drive the whole way?"

"I didn't get you out of the Wastelands," said Apana, calm once more. He began to slice the tomatoes.

Kobi was a little confused. *Why isn't he being straight with me?*

"What about the others? My friends?"

"They're alive, at the moment," said Apana.

"How do you know?"

"Hendrix has seen. Don't worry."

"Hendrix?"

"Seattle's most famous son," said Apana. "Jimi?" Kobi frowned. "Never mind." Apana whistled, and a black shape floated up in front of the skylight outside. Kobi leaped back. It was the same disc-shaped drone that had hovered over the golf course. Green lights blinked along its side, and below them, blocky lettering read, "Property of GrowCycle."

"You were spying on us?" said Kobi.

"I was keeping you safe," said Apana. "Without Hendrix interfering with the air traffic signals, CLAWS drones would have grabbed you long ago. They managed to row back to the mainland, your friends." His tone contained little emotion, as if Asha and the others meant nothing to him. "I admit, I didn't have high hopes," continued Apana. "Normally the island doesn't give up its victims so easily."

The way he spoke about the place, like it was a person, made Kobi feel uneasy. He remembered how he'd felt drawn there, almost compelled. How the island seemed like an entity in its own right, calling to Kobi and seeing into his mind. Asha had said she felt the presence too.

"I heard voices," he said. "They made me jump into the water."

"Really?" said Apana. "How fascinating. The clonal organism affects all creatures mutated by Waste, connecting with them through some kind of electromagnetic signals that influence the brain. Birds, fish, any mammals or reptiles that can swim. They enter the swamp in a sort of daze, then the clonal organism takes them. Thankfully it does not affect me, being clean of Waste. But it would suggest you have suffered mutations. And yet you look very healthy to me. So what are you? I wonder. . . . The plot thickens!"

"Is that what grabbed me?" asked Kobi. "A . . . clonal organism?"

"Indeed," said Apana. "It covers almost the entire island, connected via an underground root system—my theory is that it needs its prey to survive. It feeds off them."

"And it's Waste infected too?" said Kobi.

"I think it's the Waste in its purest form," said Apana. "Which makes sense, don't you think?"

Kobi swallowed. "I saw things too," he said. "It seemed to know my memories, my deepest fear, I think." *And my greatest hope. Seeing Dad again.*

Apana's eyes gained a glimmer of light. "How interesting. What's more interesting is that, somehow, you're still alive. Someone with such prolonged exposure, at such high concentration—you should have died almost instantly. Which goes back to my previous question. What are you, my boy?"

"I'm immune," said Kobi. "To the Waste. It doesn't affect me." Apana set down one plate in front of Kobi, then another. "You don't seem surprised," said Kobi.

The old man shrugged. He took out two glasses from a cabinet and filled up a water jug from a sink. "I'd come to the same conclusion. I hope you don't mind, but I took some of your blood while you were unconscious. I had a hard time getting the needle out."

Kobi did mind, but since the man had saved his life it felt wrong to complain. "I heal. Fast. It's a mutation from the Waste."

"Of course." Apana held the water jug still, lost for a moment. "The Waste never ceases to amaze me." His detached tone brought Kobi a spark of irritation.

The people it killed didn't find it so amazing. The people you killed!

"The equipment I have here is hardly up-to-date," said Apana, opening a jangling cutlery drawer, "but from the experiments on your blood, it appears you carry antibodies that neutralize the Waste. I'd like to run a few more tests—"

"I'm done being prodded at," Kobi said. "I need to go back to the island. The key to a Waste cure is there, in a lab somewhere: something better than a Waste cleanser, something permanent."

Apana dropped the fork he was setting by Kobi's plate. "Cleansers? A cure, you say." Then, strangely, he chuckled. "Yes. I would say you, my boy, could provide that. In theory, your blood could be synthesized and—"

"We've already tried that. The cleansers only work for a bit."

Apana ran his hands through his thin hair, fingers trembling. "Fascinating." But the sparkle in his eyes dulled like he had suddenly been brought back to reality.

"Hales said what we needed for the cure was on the island, I think at a GrowCycle facility. You must know where it is," Kobi insisted. "You have to help me."

Apana seemed to ignore the last statement. "Hales?" he whispered, the deep lines of his forehead folding. "Jonathan Hales? He's alive?"

"He was," said Kobi quietly. "He died about six months ago, helping me escape from CLAWS."

Apana let out a long breath. "Who exactly *are* you?" he repeated.

"Can you get me back to the island or not?"

Apana threw a towel over the bowl of sliced tomatoes. "Lunch can wait a few more minutes," he said. "Let me show you something."

They went back up the stairs, and Apana stood in the door of the bedroom where Kobi had woken up. In the warm glow of the afternoon light, Apana's face looked only more wrinkled, a network of deep, scarred shadows.

"My grandson's room," he said. "It seemed the most appropriate for a"—he looked Kobi up and down—"well, a boy, I suppose."

He walked along the hall, then reached up for a hatch in the ceiling and pushed it. A mechanism sprang the hatch open, and a handle appeared. Apana pulled down an extendable ladder leading into a loft. He climbed up gingerly, and Kobi could hear the creaking of his joints. "Watch your head," said the old man.

Kobi followed and found himself in a large attic space lit by two skylights and outfitted like a lab. Apart from the biohazard suit hanging outside, the room was the first sign of modernity he'd seen, with workbenches covered in circuit boards and wiring and various diagnostic tools with screens. A silver device like a small football lay on the desk, a control panel open on its side. There was a primitive hologram projector also. Along one wall a huge glass panel sealed off a smaller portion of the room, with its own air lock chamber. Inside were several specimen tanks plus racks containing vials of various fluids as well as an array of biology equipment like a microscope and a centrifuge. Apana opened one of the skylights and beckoned Kobi closer.

Kobi stared out the window, trying to work out what he was seeing. Beyond the hedge that circled the yard, he could see a vast black landscape: a decaying mass constantly slithering and moving, the air thick with spores. Trees shooting up to the sky before rotting in an instant. *The clonal organism . . . how?* A layer of mist hung over a lake beyond. Peeking through, many miles away, Kobi saw the familiar skyline of Old Seattle, with skyscrapers like silhouettes. It couldn't be an illusion.

"We're still on Mercer Island," he mumbled. "Still in the Wastelands. How?" But before Apana answered, Kobi remembered where he had seen this yard before, and everything began to fall into place, piece by piece, into one mesmerizing whole. He had to say it out loud, one step at a time. "This is the yard from that GrowCycle commercial for the launch of GAIA. I thought it was all just computer generated. But it was real. This greenhouse and yard are fertilized with GAIA, the real GAIA—it worked. You said it was supposed to filter pollutants out of the air. . . . GAIA filters out the Waste too, doesn't it? It keeps you safe here even though you're in the middle of the most contaminated place in the world."

"Yes. You've got it, my boy." Apana went to the cabinet and took out a small vial with a deep green liquid inside. "This is pure concentrated GAIA. Just a tiny sample of this liquid, less than a hundredth of a milliliter, and my yard was the result. My own

Eden, enclosed within a hell of my own making."

Kobi's skin felt electric as the true force of the discovery and what it meant overcame him. Suddenly he understood why Hales had wanted him to come here. The pieces of the puzzle all came together in his head. "This is it! The cure. The cleansers can neutralize Waste in people's bodies, and the GAIA can cleanse it from the environment. It will stop people from getting reinfected. I thought the cure would just give us a way to improve on the cleansers, create a real vaccine. But that's not it at all." Kobi shook his head, confused. "But, wait. . . . Why did GAIA only work here? Why did it become Waste everywhere else?"

"It didn't," said Apana, returning the vial to the cabinet.

Kobi thought of the folder Hales had found in the GrowCycle lab, the one labeled "2.0." The other folder Kobi had seen in the lab, labeled "1.3," had described testing on a chemical that had toxic and mutagenic effects—the Waste. "The version of GAIA that got released, that was an old kind. Version 1.3. You never meant to use that one. You knew it wouldn't work."

Apana's face looked completely impassive, like a statue's. "Yes," he whispered. "That is what happened. It doesn't matter now. It is done."

Kobi could hardly believe it. "How? How did the wrong version get released?"

Apana sank into a chair. His broad chest heaved with breaths wheezing through his nose. His face remained cold and flat, like a funeral mask. "We'd been testing versions of GAIA for months, and every time the trial began well before failing dramatically—as with version 1.3. I worked day and night, trying to find the key to a successful formula. And I did it. GAIA 2.0. I used it in my yard. I brought clients here: heads of corporations from around the world, NGOs, governments who bought GAIA and distributed it on the day of the launch to farmers—to use to reforest the Amazon, to provide food to famine-stricken countries. I thought we were going to save the world." He paused a moment. "Melanie Garcia thought differently."

A chill split Kobi's shoulder blades, and a well of horror filled his stomach. "*She* caused the disaster." He looked up into Apana's eyes. "Everyone thinks she tried to *stop* the launch of GAIA. They think you're to blame, and Melanie has become the most powerful person in the world. CLAWS took over all of GrowCycle's resources after the catastrophe. Melanie said she was the best person to lead the fight against the Waste. She turned CLAWS into the biggest corporation in the world."

Apana stared up at the sky. "Ah, Melanie. Always the opportunist. Yes, I keep up with the outside world sometimes. I listen on my radio. I know what she's become. I know what they think of me. The devil! The destroyer! The fool! The arrogant, evil breaker of the world."

"But why did she do it?" said Kobi. "How?"

"Melanie wished to make GAIA profitable," said Apana in a detached matter as if reciting a report. Kobi wondered if the only way the man could bear to recollect was to remove all emotion. "To price it high, make money. She was like a daughter to me in many ways. She was an orphan, you know? Quite brilliant. Always ambitious. Rebellious, foolish. She was never involved in the research and development side at GrowCycle, only business. She, Mischik, and Hales were the brightest students at Seattle University when I lectured there on bioscience. I took them under my wing. Mischik and Hales were my protégés too but declined my offer to work at GrowCycle. Only Melanie accepted. She and Hales were romantically involved. But I know they drifted apart as Melanie was consumed by her work."

Kobi felt a shock but realized he wasn't entirely surprised. Something in the way Melanie had talked about Hales suggested she knew him well, that they had a history.

"She had such great plans for the company," Apana continued. "She saw GrowCycle becoming a global corporation, the most powerful, diversifying into every field. She didn't understand my vision. GAIA was the world's savior. It should not be sold to consumers and corporations like any common product. We had no choice but to let her go. We were lining up a replacement for her. We hadn't told her yet, but she must have gotten wind. Melanie always took things rather personally, and the way she dealt with her enemies had always been ruthless. I never could have guessed what she was capable of though. I do not know if she fully understood what would happen when she switched the formula sent to all our production labs. I think—I *hope* that she just wanted to ruin me and the reputation of the company by sabotaging the launch so that it was an anticlimax. Not ruin the world by unleashing an international bio-disaster."

"She changed the formula of GAIA 2.0 to that of GAIA 1.3," said Kobi, horrified.

Apana nodded.

"But what about the researchers who saw the garden? They knew the truth."

"It didn't matter. Not when the Waste had already begun to ravage the world. They thought it went wrong later, like all the previous versions had, that the chemical changed, became corrupted somehow. Melanie never said anything. I suppose it was too late for her to turn back. She was happy for me to take the blame."

Kobi shook his head, trying to wrap his mind around everything. "The world thinks you're dead. They thought you died in the launch."

Apana shook his head sadly. "I was watching from here when the launch took place. I wanted to be on my own, reveling in my genius. I suppose you could say it was pride. My family was out with the spectators watching, but I stood in this attic, watching from this very window. I knew it was the best view in the city. It was. Now I cannot erase what I saw that day. The crippled, diseased trees spawning and dying; the people screaming; the helicopters falling from the sky as the spores exploded into the air, poisoning the pilots, spreading to the rest of the city and creating great living vines reaching up to the sky and mutating animals.

Instead of saving the world, GrowCycle had destroyed it."

"We need to tell people. Why didn't you try to get out, send a message?"

Apana closed his eyes. "I haven't spoken to another human in decades. This is very odd for me. Why would I wish to leave here after what I have done? Even if I wanted to, how would I? I am an old man. I cannot survive out there in the wild, with those man-eating trees and ferocious giant animals. And the communications infrastructure in the city has been destroyed. We're off the grid—all I have is my little radio."

"But CLAWS is evil. They created me in a test tube—there are loads of us—and they contaminated us with Waste as embryos. Experiments. They tried to kill me when they knew about my blood. They don't want a cure. In New Seattle, Mischik was leading a rebellion against CLAWS. But they found him. They destroyed Sol's base."

Apana nodded. "I have been hearing the news. Poor Alex. I suspect he is dead."

"Sol isn't dead though. I'm still here. And I have a mission. We have to stop CLAWS. We have to get the truth out there. We have to get GAIA 2.0 to New Seattle and the world. The Waste will be eradicated!"

"It won't help," said Apana bitterly. Kobi wanted to argue, but Apana placed both hands on his knees, and with a groan of exertion pushed himself to his feet. "Come. Let's eat. You must be hungry."

"Fine," said Kobi, after a moment. His mind was swirling with everything he had learned, and as much as he wanted to shake Apana, make him see that he couldn't hide here forever, he realized that Apana was broken. Convincing him would be difficult. Kobi would have to bide his time. But all the while, his friends were out in the Wastelands. What if they thought Kobi was dead? And New Seattle was on a ticking clock—who knew how long it had until the Waste lurking beneath it spread through the city?

Back bowed, the old man crossed the lab and descended the stairs, leaving Kobi by the skylight. He remained there, staring out at the overgrown ruins of the city. He made his way to the hatch but paused before he reached it. There was a table at the end of the attic, draped in a white sheet. Out of curiosity, Kobi pulled back the cover. The tabletop beneath was pockmarked with thousands of tiny holes. An early hologram generator. On one edge of the table there was a switch. Kobi pressed it. The rim of the table lit up, and a holographic image flickered into life on top. It was an intricately detailed, 3D image of Old Seattle before the Waste, with tiny skyscrapers, winding freeways, parks and roads, and the blue expanses of the bay. The view rotated, then the projection zoomed in on Mercer Island, dominated by a great park full of exotic trees. It focused again, on what Kobi recognized as the house in which they were standing. Children ran around the gardens, which spilled out into lush green fields. The image centered more tightly on a man in a white suit, holding an apple in his hand. His smiled and began to speak.

"*Welcome to Apana Park, birthplace of GAIA. I'm Dr. Alan Apana. The next chapter of the human race starts here. . . .*"

Kobi switched it off.

It sure did.

The food was simple but incredible. Crisp, fresh vegetables; fruit that exploded with sweetness; eggs from the chickens Apana kept in his garden. With Hales, back at the school, their diet had been repetitive: a mixture of scavenged canned goods from across the city or rehydrated food packs. At the Sol base, they'd been able to get produce from the slums but nothing like this.

"Does all this come from your garden?" asked Kobi.

"It grows quicker than I can pick it," said Apana. "You said that you were created by CLAWS. Tell me more. And how it is that you know Jonathan. Please—we have all the time in the world." He smiled.

No, we don't, thought Kobi, but he kept the thought to himself for now. And he told Apana not just his own tale but where he fit into the whole story of the Waste. He started with the CLAWS experiments with Waste-infected embryos, the mutations at Healhome, his life with Hales in the old city. Apana didn't interrupt, but when Kobi began to talk about Melanie and his kidnapping by CLAWS, he noted a tightening of Apana's facial muscles. He skimmed quickly through the remainder of his tale, all the way to the escape as the Sol base was overrun.

"And so we came here, looking for the GAIA research Hales had pointed to. That's about it."

Apana was silent for a while, then began to clear away the plates. With his back to Kobi at the sink, he spoke.

"Hales was always exceptional. So different from Melanie. She'd say she saw the bigger picture, but Jonathan was single minded, inward looking in almost all he did. It was no wonder that Melanie made him Head of Research at CLAWS. And from what you say, I see why Jonathan ran away with you. If he believed you were the key, he would have risked everything."

"He lied to me, for years," said Kobi.

"Sometimes we have to lie to protect the ones we love," said Apana.

"I know that now," said Kobi. "It's in the past. The important thing now is that we get GAIA 2.0 back to New Seattle. Between that and the cleansers, we could wipe out the Waste for good. If the world heard the truth from you, if they could see this garden, they would believe. I know it."

Apana said nothing.

"The Waste is about to overrun the city," urged Kobi. "We can tell the world what Melanie Garcia did. We can save millions of lives."

Apana seemed to shrink into himself. "It's impossible," he said. "They would not listen to me."

"Then they'll listen to me," said Kobi. "I have the cure to the Waste in my blood. We have the power to reverse all this—to fix the entire world."

"I won't last five minutes out in the Wastelands! The predators, the living, carnivorous flora . . . I am stuck here!"

"What's wrong with you?" said Kobi. "You can fix this, I'm telling you!"

"No . . . ," said Apana. He was shaking his head over and over like his brain was stuck on a loop. "Don't you see? I trusted Melanie. All those people who died . . . It's my fault. . . . I can't—"

"Stop being a coward!" said Kobi.

Apana's head slumped between his shoulders, then he stood up, his food barely touched, and walked out into the yard.

Back up in the bedroom, Kobi's clothes had dried, so he put them on. Apana was nowhere to be seen outside, but the light was fading beyond the garden. As Kobi turned from the window, his eyes fell on the photo beside the bed of the family on the beach. He guessed from the man's wide cheekbones and strong features that he was Apana's son and the children were his grandchildren. It must have been devastating to lose them. Kobi felt a lump in his throat as he thought of Hales, so weak and sick near the end.

He reached for his bag, pulled out the photo Asha had returned to him, and then wandered back downstairs. He found Apana sitting on the porch, face bathed in shadow, smoking a cigar. Without speaking, Kobi sat down beside the old man.

"I only have one a year," said Apana, blowing smoke away. "I was rationing them, but I never thought I'd live this long."

Kobi held the photo in front of Apana. "We used to take these every year," he said. "We called them Yearbook photos." Apana chuckled, and Kobi continued. "This is the only one I have now. For a long time after I learned the truth about Dr. Hales, I hated him. I just thought of all the lies he'd told me or at least the truth he'd hidden. I know why now. He was scared of driving me away or hurting me, but I wish he had told me sooner. In the end he ran out of time." He paused. "You still have time."

Apana turned to look at him, his eyes moist. "You know, the thing that hurts me most is that I never got to say goodbye to my family. We didn't have the best relationship anyway because I was always so busy. And they died thinking I was the one who killed them."

"You can't change the past," said Kobi. "But you can still affect the future. More families will die if you lock the truth away here."

Apana looked out into the yard again, his mind impossible to read. Finally, he stubbed the cigar out on the step, placed his hands on his knees, and pried his body upright. "You're a lot like Jonathan, you know. Stubborn."

"So you'll help me get back to New Seattle?" said Kobi.

"No," said Apana, and Kobi felt suddenly deflated.

"But . . . if what you say is true, the Sol resistance has been crushed. Even if we could get back, we'd be walking right into the hands of CLAWS. They'd capture us and stop us from making any more GAIA 2.0."

"We've still got to try!" said Kobi desperately. "There's no other way!"

Apana wagged his finger. He looked rejuvenated. "Not true, son. Not true."

15

BACK IN THE ATTIC lab, Apana pointed to the Space Needle in the distance, its lights twinkling a little against the dusky sky. "It's a broadcast antenna," he said. "As you know, in the aftermath of the Waste disaster, CLAWS took over GrowCycle's labs, facilities, our resources, all our drones. GrowCycle used the Space Needle as our central comms station to control the drones spreading the GAIA over Mercer Island. We made a deal with the mayor of Seattle. They thought it would be a good promotion for the city."

Apana stared at Kobi meaningfully. Kobi had the impression he was being constantly tested every moment he spent in the man's presence. Suddenly a thought came to him. He remembered the drone bug that Spike had developed at the Sol base: it was designed to hack into the CLAWS communications network and to spread word of Horizon. "You think we could use the Space Needle to transmit a message to New Seattle? CLAWS won't block it out because it's coming from their own source."

"Exactly!" said Apana. "CLAWS still uses the original Grow-Cycle frequencies to communicate. That's how Hendrix can disrupt the Snatchers. He operates on the same network. I'll send the message out to every CLAWS app. They will all pick up the broadcast."

Kobi's skin tingled with excitement. "So we record a message, then send your drone to the Needle, then—"

"Ah, not so fast," said Apana. "We will need my voice codes to access the broadcast computer. The most important GrowCycle systems could only be accessed by very senior people—me and Melanie and a few others. We'll have to get there in person, and we'll have to hope the voice activation still works."

All Kobi could say was, "Oh." The plan suddenly looked a lot less likely to succeed. "Do you think you can make it?"

Apana shrugged. "With your help, perhaps." He grinned. "About time I took a trip, don't you think?"

In the backyard, they stood in front of Hendrix, the GrowCycle drone, and watched the holographic footage they'd filmed—their message to the outside world. Kobi had gone first.

"CLAWS is lying to you. They don't want you to get better. They don't want a cure to the Waste. My name is Kobi Hales. I'm immune

to the Waste—thanks to CLAWS experiments. And my blood will help cure it forever. CLAWS tried to kill me, but I managed to escape. . . ."

"Do you think it will work?" Apana asked as the recording continued.

"If enough people see it," said Kobi. His section ended, and Apana's holographic image took center stage.

"And I'm Dr. Alan Apana, founder of GrowCycle. Everything you were told about me is a lie." The projection held up a vial of clear liquid. *"This is GAIA 2.0, the formula I spent my life working on. The outbreak of the contagion you call "Waste" was a criminal act carried out by the current head of CLAWS, Melanie Garcia. . . ."*

Together they watched until the end, where the drone showed footage of Apana's garden amid the barren landscape of the Waste. The message could have been longer, but there was no saying if CLAWS would be able to detect it and block it. They needed to get the point across quickly.

"Are you ready?" asked Kobi.

"No," said Apana, managing a smile. "I think we're almost certain to die."

Kobi didn't particularly like the feeling of leaving the idyllic gardens of Apana's home. But he didn't want to wait. Every second that passed increased the chance of his friends giving up on him. And he couldn't forget the Waste contamination below New

Seattle: it only needed access to the surface, a way out, and the whole city would be gripped in a second disaster.

They gathered supplies—food, water, makeshift weapons, blankets, a large ax Apana used for firewood, and his hunting rifle—and loaded the truck. Last of all, Apana placed a number of bushy potted plants on the back seat of the jeep and in the foot wells. "Lavender, camellia, euonymus," he said. "Apart from the lovely smells, they are natural air filterers. The GAIA in their xylem will counteract the Waste spores in the air." He was back in his hazmat suit, and he took the driver's seat, Kobi taking the passenger.

"Ready?" said Apana from behind his mask.

Kobi nodded, strapping himself in. He tried to keep calm. He knew once they got back out into the terrain of the clonal organism, its strange effects would overcome him again. Apana didn't have a second hazmat suit.

The doctor started the engine. He pressed a button on the car radio, and the speakers played a light summery tune that Kobi recognized as "Wouldn't It Be Nice" by The Beach Boys. Apana drummed along on the steering wheel, whistling, as he released the hand brake.

The car rumbled along the gravel path toward the front of the yard. Hendrix flew ten feet above them at the same speed. Out in the Wastelands, the drone would blind any nearby Snatchers with its interference signal. Gravel crunched below. The vast hedges rose up before them, and soon the jeep entered a dark green passage through them. Rows of sprinklers sent a constant spray across the dark, forested tunnel.

"GAIA is diluted with the water," said Apana, turning on the windshield wipers. "The sprinkler system is set up all over the yard. The organisms filter out the Waste from the air naturally, and the water is a safeguard against active exposure—it neutralizes any large invasions of spores or animals." The path through the hedges was around twenty feet long and ended in a cast-iron gate. Apana stopped the jeep in front of it. Kobi stared. Beyond the gate, creeping tentacles dripping with sludgy decay curled up the railings. But as they reached through, they froze, their slippery black forms turning solid and woody; they sprouted healthy-looking mushrooms, moss, and even small ivy flowers. *Neutralized by the GAIA.* The healthy organisms fell back into the writhing pool of sludge, disappearing beneath the carpet of moving roots.

"The boundary of life and death," Apana said, meeting Kobi's eye with a manic grin as he pressed a button on a small plastic remote. The gate began to creak open. "Time to enter the underworld."

Apana revved the jeep and powered it into the sludgy, black, slithering terrain of the clonal organism, the tires of the truck bumping over the constantly moving ground. Kobi glanced back at the potted plants on the back seat, hoping they could keep the air mostly filtered, but soon the voice came back, ghostly and distant but haunting Kobi's mind with doubt.

You belong here. You belong with us. Spawn of Waste. Join us.

The 4x4's headlights shone twin beams over the barren landscape. "Love this album," said Apana as "You Still Believe in Me" came on the car stereo. "Reminds me of my surfing days." He seemed oblivious to the evil mass of putrid living decay clawing at the windows and slamming down on the ceiling of the car with scraping thuds.

Kobi pointed to a bulbous growth expanding from the ground. When it reached the size of a small boulder, it exploded, sending a dense mass of black dust over the windshield. Apana sprayed the glass with cleaner fluid and ramped up the wipers. "Wretched spore sacs," he said.

"What are they?"

"The clonal organism creates them as a way to reproduce—like a mushroom or fir tree does. Those spores are what first carried the Waste to the other side of the lake, spreading it through the ecosystem as it was absorbed and passed on by trees and animals, in less concentrated forms. Oh, watch out!" The car rolled as they hit another of the sacs, sending another dense cloud of spores over the side of the truck.

"Gets a bit tricky around the center of the clonal organism," said Apana. "This is where most of the sacs are. You know, I believe that beneath the earth there is an entire lake of these spores. Quite worrying."

Apana seemed a master at working the truck through the terrain. He simply revved harder if they got stuck or rolled the steering wheel around a clump of roots—or the spore sacs or a carcass of a giant bat, its leathery wings constricted in the grip of a slimy branch of thorns. Its great white eyes were slowly sucked into the ground.

Soon the jeep broke out into light on the banks of the island. They arrived shortly at an old boathouse on the shore.

"I used to love sailing on Lake Washington," said Apana. "All water sports were my thing, but it's a bit cold for surfing around here and no waves, of course! Waterskiing. Now that's a rush. It used to be that on a good day, there'd be hundreds of boats out there."

Staring out over the mist-covered expanse of stagnant water, Kobi found that *very* hard to imagine.

"Ah, here we are." Apana's boat was a twenty-foot sailing vessel. It too was covered in a film of dusty black spores.

They exited the truck, and immediately Kobi felt a swell of panic rise up and the voice of the Waste louder in his ears. *Come back. Come back to us. . . .* He saw strange movements under the water. Hallucinations. He blinked, ignoring them. Apana, unaffected, led Kobi along a dock toward the boat. "I haven't taken the *Nurturer* out for a spin in twenty years, you know. But I must say I am glad to see her again. And look: not even any mold. I suppose the concentrated Waste kills it too fast. Remarkable, isn't it?"

Keep a clear head, Kobi told himself as his heart raced and his eyes went moist with the toxicity of the air. Kobi had to help Apana on board. Though he didn't know a thing about sailing, he followed Apana's instructions, and they were soon tacking slowly over the water under a light breeze. It felt good to see the island retreating behind him into the mist. Hendrix was conserving power, resting beside the tiller—Apana said the GrowCycle drone's charging capacity had dipped over the years, and he couldn't find any compatible battery cells or fix the ones currently installed.

They followed a bearing given by the drone, aiming for the last known location of Asha and the others—and almost as soon as the far bank was in sight, Kobi spotted a small fire on the hillside above.

"There they are!" he shouted.

Asha must have sensed him because she came running down to the shore with Fionn and Yaeko behind her. Apana ordered Kobi to turn into the wind and lower the sails, and he dropped the anchor.

Asha stared around at the water, clearly checking for danger, then waded out to the boat. "Kobi! What happened? Are you okay? Where did you get the boat?"

Kobi grinned and with one heave hoisted her over the gunwale and on board. "Yes to all of those questions. Except 'what happened,' and you're never going to believe me when I answer that." She hugged him. Yaeko scurried up on deck and gave Fionn a hand up.

"We thought you were dead!" Asha said to Kobi.

Even Yaeko looked pleased to see him, tapping him awkwardly on the arm. "Back from the dead, Caveman. You know you really took us by surprise when you jumped overboard. Bold move. We thought you were toast."

"I would have been," said Kobi. "If it wasn't for him."

Apana stepped out from the back of the boat, making the others jump in shock. "Meet Dr. Alan Apana," said Kobi.

None of the Wastelings moved an inch. Apana gave a small smile. "Greetings."

"*The* Alan Apana?" said Yaeko. "The guy who caused all this?"

"I can explain that," said the old man.

"It was Melanie," said Kobi. "She caused the Waste disaster. She was about to be fired from GrowCycle and switched GAIA 2.0—the one that *worked*—with an old, failed version, which turned into the Waste. Apana didn't have any idea what she was planning."

Asha's eyes shone. "A working GAIA?"

"Hales was right!" Kobi answered, grinning. "GAIA 2.0 really works—I've seen it with my own eyes. That garden from the GrowCycle commercial was real. It filters Waste naturally. It's the cure! Think about it. A way to cleanse the Waste from the environment so once people are treated with the cleansers, they'll never get reinfected. We've been thinking about it all wrong. The cure isn't just a vaccine. It's a way to purify the entire world!" Kobi explained Apana's plan to use the Space Needle to broadcast their message to everyone with a CLAWS app, and Asha, Fionn, and Yaeko nodded, taking it all in.

Apana began to remove his bio-suit. "It's a clever plan. But it does rely on my not keeling over." He coughed. "You don't mind administering a dose of the Horizon to this poor old man? Otherwise this suit will slow me down. Not that I can get much slower."

"Of course," muttered Asha.

She prepared the dose, passing the syringe to Apana. As soon as he'd administered it, his face glowed. "I feel better than ever!" He sniffed the air and looked around. "It really is remarkable to be out here."

Kobi saw Asha tensing her jaw in anger. He knew what she must be thinking. *It wasn't remarkable for the millions the Waste killed.* Melanie might have caused the Waste disaster, but Apana had played a part too, even if it was unintentional.

"How do we avoid the Snatchers?" Yaeko asked. "You said the Space Needle is where they, like, roost? Seems like a bit of a problem. A lot of a problem, actually."

"Ah," said Apana. "Hendrix!"

The drone rose from the deck of the boat, making everyone jump again, but Kobi held up a hand. "It's okay—he's on our side. He operates on the same frequency as the Snatchers. He scrambles their signals."

Kobi pulled out his map and laid it on the deck. It had gotten soaked when he'd jumped into the lake. He'd dried it out by the fire at Apana's mansion, but the pencil marks were faded—not that they mattered now. Hales's landmarks weren't important. The map wasn't for surviving now or finding any labs. They just had to get to one location. He traced a path with his finger from their current position, up Lake Washington, and around the north of Old Seattle, looping back south to the west coast of downtown, near the waterfront where Kobi, Asha, and Fionn had first found Hales's secret lab. From there it was only a few blocks farther to the Space Needle. Kobi showed the others the route. "We'll sail most of the way. Hendrix keeps the Snatchers from seeing us, but most of us should stay belowdecks to limit heat signals."

"Quite a sail," said Apana. "I'll take the tiller, shall I? I'll call you up when we need to tack, but we should be running with the wind until we turn west." Kobi helped him hoist the sail, then joined the others belowdecks in a musty cabin. As the boat rolled, pans rattled in cupboards. Kobi took out a knife sharpener and ran the steel over the edge of the ax that he'd brought from Apana's until its edge was razor-thin.

"I thought axes were my style," said Asha. Kobi remembered the blunt hatchet they'd scavenged in the underpass last time they were in Old Seattle; how Asha had used the weapon to hold off the attack of the rats.

Kobi smiled. "This time it's mine. You've got the stun baton. Keep your senses alert for any animals. I don't fancy meeting another orca. And Fionn, we might need you to keep things away."

Fionn was staring out a porthole. Kobi felt a wave of sorrow from him and headed over, but before he could speak, Fionn said, "You want to kill the Waste. I won't have any powers." Tears were brimming in his eyes.

Asha was watching them with a concerned expression, but Kobi shook his head at her. "You lived without them before," said Kobi, turning back to Fionn. "It has to be done."

Fionn nodded. "When I saw you jump into the water, I was scared," he said. "I felt helpless. It made me realize how Asha must feel watching the Waste consume me." He pointed to Asha, Yaeko, Kobi, then to himself. He said out loud, "Home is us."

Kobi smiled. "Right. We'll all be together. Whatever happens afterward. If we ever defeat CLAWS, we stay together. We'll have each other. We're a family."

"So now you're back to speaking out loud all the time?" Asha teased.

Fionn shrugged, cheeks flushing slightly. "I need to get used it. Being *normal.*" He rolled his eyes.

"You are not normal," said Yaeko, and everyone laughed.

The sail took two hours. Kobi occasionally scuttled out on deck to help Apana maneuver. Apana was smoking another cigar and seemed to be thoroughly enjoying the expedition. "I just saw a salmon the size of a great white!" he shouted at one point, with another manic grin.

When they curved around the north of the island, Kobi called the others up to watch gigantic bats roosting under the broken end section of the bridge. "Fionn," Kobi said nervously. "Can you . . . ?"

Apana reached for the hunting rifle resting in the cockpit, aiming it at the bats, but Fionn pulled his arm down. The fair-haired boy held up his hand, and the bats simply stared down watching. The end of the bridge was covered in hanging creeper ivy, jagged thorns blocking the way ahead, but Fionn made them slither aside. Apana's cigar almost dropped out of his mouth. "You kids really are something special," he mumbled.

As they neared their landing point, Kobi found if he glanced back to the southwest he could see West Seattle Bridge. Somewhere beyond where the bridge reached West Seattle, concealed by a thick patch of heavy forest, was Bill Gates High School. When all this was over—and if they were still alive—he promised himself he'd go back there. Even if the memories were painful.

Finally, Apana steered the boat to a jetty, and Kobi and Yaeko tied it up. There were twenty long wooden jetties stretching out from the rock harbor side. Downtown Seattle rose up before them—a forest of giant trees, like a barricade, the colossal trunks sending the sounds of the harbor echoing back to them: waves slapping against the hulls of discarded boats, the honks of a few seals reverberating through the night air. Kobi tried to ignore the sinking fear that the rippling water brought out in his stomach.

Kobi glanced at the map, gray and faint in his night vision, and they headed inland. Asha went first, sensing for danger, Fionn behind her, ready to control any hostile Waste organisms. Kobi accompanied Apana, occasionally allowing the old man to lean on his shoulder. Yaeko followed at the rear, muttering fearfully, her skin changed to a dusky blue-black to camouflage herself. Overhead, Hendrix whirred. Already the lights of Snatchers could be seen above, flying to and from the towering spire of the Space

Needle. *I just hope that thing works*, Kobi thought, watching the small old GrowCycle drone.

As they moved carefully through the city blocks, scurrying between giant Douglas firs and silver birch and beating through the coarse grass breaking through the broken roads, Kobi organized them each to watch in a different direction so they had their whole perimeter covered. When he heard any signs of movement—birds rustling in the trees or the rumble of tremors beneath their feet—he would check with Asha.

"No Chokers. Only some raccoons nearby and a few rats. Fionn can deal with those."

"I can deal with Chokers too," said Fionn.

But ten paces on, Asha stopped beside him quite suddenly. "Don't move," she whispered.

The others had frozen. "Cougars," said Apana.

Three big cats, one enormous and two smaller, were standing directly ahead. Even the younger ones stood almost as tall as Kobi. The largest, which must have been the mother, eyed them, her muzzle wrinkling into a snarl. Kobi could see every one of her ribs. With a growl, she left the two cubs behind and padded a few strides in their direction.

Apana lifted his rifle from his shoulder.

"Don't," said Fionn, breaking from the group and standing in front of Apana. "She's just curious."

"Really? Because she looks hungry," said Yaeko.

"Move," said Apana.

Fionn remained where he was.

The cougar padded closer but stopped a careful distance away. Her eyes were sickly yellow with Waste as she looked between them. She cocked her head as her gaze settled on Fionn. *Either he's talking to her, or she's looking for the weakest one to attack,* Kobi thought.

Fionn moved nearer still—took another step, then another. He looked tiny beside the big cat.

Kobi drew a sharp breath as the young boy reached out and touched the cougar's face, ruffling its fur with his fingers. The big cat tossed her head, licking his hand. Fionn's lips were moving, but there was no sound, and the cougar straightened up sharply before turning around and walking back toward her cubs. Apana's bearded jaw hung low. "I've never seen . . ."

Fionn still faced away from them, watching the mother rejoin her young. Kobi had never come across cubs in the Wastelands before. Hales had often said he thought infected animals were infertile, unable to breed, but he must have been wrong. This was a family, or at least part of one.

With that realization came a prickling sensation along the back of Kobi's neck. As Fionn turned around, the look of happiness of his face dropped away. In almost the same instant Asha drew a gasp. Kobi spun around to see another cougar running toward them on heavy paws. Bigger even than the female, it had ragged fur that was torn and bare in patches, its eyes bloodshot. One leg was gone, and half of its face had been eaten away by disease, exposing its jawbone and rotten teeth. But it closed the gap impossibly fast. Its gaze set on Yaeko.

16

KOBI HEARD THE RIFLE crack, and the creature jerked—but kept coming. Kobi threw himself into its path, swinging the ax and feeling it bite into flesh. The weight of the creature knocked him off his feet, and searing pain flared from his leg. The cougar's bulk slammed into the ground beside him. At once blood began to pool beneath it, and he realized his ax was embedded in the big cat's flank. There was a bullet hole in its neck as well.

But Kobi was bleeding too, from three deep slices across his thigh. He almost retched at the sight of his own flesh torn open. Asha rushed toward him, throwing down her pack and pulling out a roll of bandages. She pushed a bandage hard against his wound. The others congregated around him, and Fionn looked completely distraught. "It's okay, Kobi," Asha was saying. "It's going to be okay."

"*I didn't see it coming*," Fionn said, weak with shock.

"None of us did," Kobi bit out. The pain came in waves, and the bandage was already soaked through. "It's not your fault."

"They were hunting us," said Yaeko. "They tricked us."

The massive male was still breathing very softly, but its eyes were closed. Apana stood over it and aimed his rifle for a point-blank shot. Fionn jumped as the old man put the creature out of its misery.

"What now?" said Apana. "We can't go on."

"I'll be fine," said Kobi. As Asha lifted the bandage away and replaced it with a fresh one, he was relieved to see that the blood seeping from the claw marks was already clotting. It still hurt though. Asha tied off the bandage and got back to her feet.

"Kobi's right," she said. "We haven't come this far just to turn back."

Kobi winced with every step at first. They walked along what had once been 6th Avenue, the Space Needle clearly in sight, Snatchers drifting to and fro all around it. Apana activated his drone's scrambler, and they kept close beneath it while also sticking to the very edge of the road, where the vegetation that clung to the bases of the former office buildings at least offered partial concealment. None of the Snatchers came directly toward their position, but Kobi caught occasional glimpses of their menacing shapes moving across the intersections.

It felt completely wrong to Kobi—for years the Snatchers had been the single most dangerous hazard in the city, and Hales's first rule was to hide if he ever saw one. And if he couldn't hide, run. Yet here they were, heading right into the highest concentration of the deadly drones he'd ever seen. No doubt CLAWS had cameras on each and every one, so if the scrambler failed and they were spotted, any one of them could relay their location back to CLAWS.

The Space Needle loomed large ahead as they reached the end of the street. On the map, a park surrounded the base of the tower, threaded with footpaths. Now it was a meadow filled with a riot of exotic wildflowers of every color. Hales had told him the Needle had been the city's foremost tourist attraction in the days before the Waste.

"There's an elevator in the spine of the tower," said Apana.

"Will it be working?" asked Asha.

Apana nodded. "It should be. The entire tower was fitted with solar cells—part of GrowCycle's green image."

"How can we get there?" asked Yaeko. "There's no cover. We can't just run across."

"We have to trust Hendrix," said Apana. "Hendrix, proximity one," he said, and the drone drifted right over his head. "As long as he's switched on, the scramblers will keep us hidden."

"Are you sure?" said Yaeko.

"I'm a scientist," said Apana. "I'm never completely sure."

"Okay," said Kobi. "We don't really have a choice. Here goes. Stay close together."

They moved in a tight group, right out in the open. Kobi kept his eyes fixed on the sky, looking for any indication they'd been detected. It would only take one drone to spot them, and the rest would come in a swarm; they'd have no chance at all. But there were no obvious patterns in the flight paths of the Snatchers, and none came close to ground level, instead zipping off to other parts of the city. Now that they were nearer the base of the Space Needle, Kobi saw there were hundreds of the drones clinging dormant to the central spire of the landmark like larvae ready to hatch from a nest.

They arrived at a glass door leading into a lobby area. Inside it was a blanket of moss and flowers and ivy covering various tourist signs pointing to a gift shop, lavatories, and a café. Kobi pushed the door open, and they crossed the empty space to a bank of elevators. Just as Apana had promised, the doors opened almost as soon as he pressed the button to summon the elevator. The five of them climbed aboard, and Hendrix floated in beside them. "Hendrix, deactivate," said Apana, and the drone came to rest on the floor at his feet. Apana pressed the topmost button for the "Observation Deck."

The elevator was glass sided, and as it began to climb, Kobi watched the city drop away. He turned away from the ranks of sleeping Snatchers to look out over the sweep of the bay. The plant life stopped abruptly at the ragged shoreline, like it had been torn off by some giant hand, with wrecks of ships and buildings half submerged. The sea was black and choppy and completely unwelcoming.

The elevator opened into an expansive room with a curved outer wall of glass giving a 360-degree view of the city. But Apana didn't seem interested, turning instead to a bank of keyboards and monitors on the inner wall. First he scanned his fingerprints, and the screen lit up.

"Greetings, Dr. Apana. Voice identification, please."

"ID Code Alpha, Alpha," said Apana.

Now all the monitors blinked into life, in addition to holographic displays showing 3D maps of the city, with tiny red lights representing the drones.

"*Readings indicate critical failure of environmental containment*," said the computer. "*Recommend emergency evacuation and quarantine protocols.*"

"A bit late for that," muttered Apana, his fingers moving stiffly over the touch pads. "Hendrix, connect via VCP to port three." The drone floated close and spun. Something began to whir inside it. "The upload should only take a few . . ." Hendrix made a beeping sound. "There! Now we just have to transmit." He continued to type, then tapped the screen triumphantly. "It's done," he said. The message began to play.

"CLAWS is lying to you. They don't want you to get better. They don't want a cure to the Waste. My name is Kobi Hales. I'm immune to—"

Hendrix wobbled a little in the air. "*Charge at ten percent*," said an electronic voice. *"Sleep mode activating."* The green lights dimmed, and the drone lowered to the ground.

Apana's features shifted from happiness to dread in a flash. "Negative, Hendrix. Stay awake."

The drone rose once more.

"Um . . . does that count as switching off?" said Asha.

"We should be okay," said Apana. "It was only for a split second."

Yaeko shook her head. "Oh no . . . Look!"

On the holograph display, the red dots showing the locations of the Snatchers were moving in a strange pattern, wheeling around in the sky and coalescing into a swarm. Slowly they began to stream back toward the Space Needle. Kobi glanced outside and saw them, all of them, closing in on the Observation Deck. The sky seemed to darken as the winged drones blocked the view.

The message was still playing Kobi's words when something thumped into the roof above their heads.

"They're coming!" he cried.

17

MORE SNATCHERS SLAMMED DOWN above them, hitting the roof of the tower. The Observation Deck trembled with each impact.

Then, farther around the viewing platform, glass exploded inward. A Snatcher reached inside, gripping the vertical steel stanchions that separated the glass panes. It tried to squeeze its body through, but it wouldn't quite fit. The Snatcher screeched and retreated, then flung itself again, crumpling the metal and falling through the gap it had created. It righted itself on its insectoid legs and turned its visual sensors in their direction. A series of beeps sounded, perhaps summoning others, then it lumbered toward them.

"Back into the elevator!" shouted Asha, stabbing at the button. The doors remained stubbornly closed.

"Run!" said Kobi, grabbing Fionn and practically dragging

him away. Apana stumbled after them too, with Asha at his side. Only Yaeko remained, frozen in place. The Snatcher lunged for her, but she jumped above its stinger, clinging to the ceiling. The drone turned and reached upward, and she fired the stun baton. The Snatcher crashed into the wall and lay still. The elevator doors pinged open. But before they could climb in, two more Snatchers came scurrying along the Observation Deck.

They all ran in the opposite direction.

"Hendrix, Omega Protocol in three," said Apana.

"What's Omega Protocol?" asked Kobi.

"You'll see," said the old man.

Just as the two Snatchers reached the floating droid, it exploded with a colossal boom that shattered a dozen or more windowpanes and set Kobi's ears ringing. When the smoke cleared, all that remained of the Snatchers were tangles of charred metal. Unfortunately, the explosion had wiped out the wall console as well.

"Did the message finish?" asked Yaeko, aghast.

"I don't know. Most of it got out. That's what matters," said Apana. "There's another elevator on the far side. We need to get to it before—"

A Snatcher lurched toward them from the opposite direction. Kobi readied his ax, looking for an opening as it advanced. He swung and caught one leg, but another swiped him in the stomach and threw him against the wall. Through a winded daze, he saw the Snatcher move toward Fionn, who was completely unarmed in its path. Kobi was sure he'd be trampled, until Asha shoved Fionn aside. Then she screamed as the Snatcher's claw stabbed down at her back. Kobi was relieved to see its blow land squarely on her backpack—but as she fell, he saw blood coming from her shoulder. The Snatcher had stabbed all the way through.

Asha lay helpless on the ground. The Snatcher reared back, ready to finish her, but Kobi managed to throw himself shoulder first into its back, knocking it off balance. It bounced into a wall, mashing screens, then turned to face him, lashing out with a claw. Kobi ducked beneath it, then lifted the ax double-handed and brought it down as hard as he could right in the center of the creature's "forehead." Sparks showered over him as the Snatcher's legs spasmed, its central motor systems malfunctioning. He yanked the ax clear, then cut into the Snatcher's damaged part again. This time the Snatcher lay still.

Yaeko and Fionn helped Asha off the floor.

"I can stand," she said, but her face had gone pale, and she was hunched over in pain. Her pack lay spilled open on the floor.

Kobi led the way farther around the perimeter of the Observation Deck. Impacts rocked the structure on all sides as Snatchers attached themselves to the outside of the glass viewing panes and began to smash through. More piled in behind, eager to join the frenzy, but if anything, their sheer number proved an impediment. Only a handful of them got through the swarm. When Kobi and the others reached the far elevator, the doors opened almost at once. They piled in and the glass door closed. A Snatcher charged at them, and the glass splintered but didn't break as the elevator began to descend. Inside, everyone seemed to breathe out at once.

"What now?" said Yaeko. "They'll be waiting for us at the bottom."

They didn't get that far.

The elevator ground to a shuddering halt, suspended. From every side, Kobi saw Snatchers closing in. Five at first, then more than a dozen. They climbed from above and below, clinging to the steel spans like insects.

"They've stopped the elevator," said Apana.

Yaeko shrank into a corner, hugging her knees and burying her face in them. Asha shared a glance with Kobi, one hand clutching her injured shoulder, and shook her head hopelessly. The Snatchers blocked almost all the light as they swarmed across the outside of the elevator. Kobi felt their tiny gleaming eyes settle on him hungrily. Was Melanie watching now? Was she controlling them? Several extended spinning saw blades. When they touched the glass of the elevator walls, a hideous screeching flooded the enclosed space.

"This is it," Kobi said. He couldn't believe it would end like this. After getting so far, transmitting the message. Without thinking, he reached out to hold Asha's hand. If they were going to die here he didn't want to feel alone. She squeezed as well and hugged Fionn closer. Fionn's eyes were closed, but when they opened, they held no fear.

Only rage.

Glass splintered as a Snatcher sting pushed through, slicing toward Yaeko. She squirmed out of the way—straight into the grip of a claw that broke through. It clamped over her boot, pulling her toward it. "Help me!" she cried, unable to tear free.

Kobi smashed at the claw with the hilt of his ax, but another Snatcher claw knocked him off balance, and the ax slipped from his hand. Asha grabbed Yaeko's arm and pulled. For a moment the girl and the machine were locked in a tug-of-war, and Kobi scrambled to grab hold of Yaeko's other arm. Kobi felt his heels sliding across the floor, unable to prevent Yaeko being heaved away, feet-first, toward the open side of the elevator.

In a flash of white, the Snatcher was flung sideways. Asha, Kobi, and Yaeko tumbled backward in a heap. He didn't know what had happened, but then another Snatcher vanished with what sounded like a squawk. Kobi saw a long orange bill, a flap of gigantic wings, before whatever it was darted away. One by one, the other Snatchers detached from the side of the elevator, and as the view of the skyline opened up, Kobi saw more of the new arrivals. The white birds were pelicans, air gusting with each beat of their enormous wings, their beaks alone seven or eight feet long. One carried a Snatcher dangling by one leg and squirming to get free.

There were other birds too. Kobi spotted a massive hawk that swooped low and wrapped its talons around a Snatcher before crushing it and dropping its carcass into the grasslands below. Three other attack drones were in pursuit, but the hawk tipped its wings and evaded them easily before batting two aside with a powerful wing stroke. There were bats too, the flaps of their leathery wings snapping the air like whips. Enormous wasps hummed in the night, their stings stabbing into the Snatchers' circuitry, disabling them instantly. The Snatchers spun, trying to right themselves in midair before smashing into the sides of buildings and bursting into flames. Smaller birds too, sleek seabirds with dappled feathers, stabbed down from higher altitudes, taking out Snatchers left and right before a flock of pigeons arrived in a convoy over the skyscrapers. Kobi was turning in his spot, enthralled, when he finally understood what was happening. Fionn stood perfectly still in the center of the battered elevator. His eyelids were still closed, but behind them his eyes were shifting quickly. Kobi remembered Johanna's words. *Anger. Anger makes Fionn's powers stronger.*

"He's controlling them all," Kobi gasped, staring around at the birds, insects, and bats.

A stiff breeze buffeted the inside of the elevator, streaming through the smashed wall panels and stirring Fionn's hair. The Snatchers were in disarray, changing directions to face the oncoming threats. One by one they were picked off, either knocked from the sky by wings and beaks or seized in a raptor's talons and carried away. Kobi saw several Snatchers latch on to the wings of a hawk. It flapped in panic, but another clamped on to the side of its head. The giant bird of prey let out a screech of rage as one of its wings buckled. More Snatchers flung themselves onto its body. From the elevator Kobi watched as the majestic bird careened through the sky above them and into the Observation Deck. The impact reverberated down the shaft, and suddenly the elevator gave an ominous creak. One of the cables above snapped, and the car tipped sharply. Apana was thrown toward the opening in one of the walls, but Kobi managed to grab his wrist and hold on. The others braced themselves, Yaeko clinging to the wall with both hands, and even Fionn's eyes sprang open in surprise.

"It's going to fall!" said Yaeko. "We've got to get out of here."

Easier said than done, thought Kobi. There was no way to climb down that he could see. Heading upward through the shaft might be a possibility for Yaeko, but Kobi wasn't sure how far he'd make it, and the others would find it impossible. Could he carry them if he had to?

He felt a hand on his arm. It was Fionn, teeth gritted, brow furrowed in concentration and fury. *"I have a way, Kobi,"* he said. *"They're coming."*

"What's coming?" asked Kobi. He looked out through the aerial dogfight still raging between the flying animals of the Wastelands and the Snatchers. A fluorescent-green, glimmering craft was winding a steady path from the south, looping between the skyscrapers of downtown Seattle. It looked at first like a kind of futuristic airship, the shape of a narrow barge and sparkling with light, but as it came toward them Kobi realized it had two huge pairs of wings oscillating at such tremendous speed they were just a blur.

"It's a dragonfly!" exclaimed Asha.

The creature had two bulbous yellow eyes on the side of its head and delicate legs dangling under its body, lined with fur. It cut a path through the airborne battle, and the buzz of its wings became a deafening drone. Rotating in midair, the tip of its stiff, segmented abdomen swung around until it came to rest against the edge of the leaning elevator.

"*Climb on*," said Fionn.

"You must be kidding," said Yaeko.

But Asha scrambled on right away, shuffling with her legs on either side of the long tail. Kobi helped Apana to the edge, supporting the old man as he clambered on as well.

In small cautious steps, Yaeko straddled the insect and lowered her body to its abdomen, wrapping her arms around the insectoid body. She looked like she was going to be sick. The elevator jerked another few inches.

"Quickly!" yelled Kobi, giving her a shove. He jumped on behind her. The skin of the dragonfly felt curiously soft, like worn leather. He reached back, holding out a hand for Fionn. Just as their fingers touched, the elevator groaned, shuddered, and then fell. He gripped Fionn's hand; the sudden dead weight almost pulled him off the dragonfly's back. Yelping in terror, Fionn swung from Kobi's grip, dangling over a drop of hundreds of feet. The elevator slammed into the ground far below, throwing up a cloud of debris and dust. Kobi gritted his teeth and hauled Fionn up beside him. As soon as Fionn was seated, they lurched off through the air.

Kobi could do nothing but hold on, leaning closely over the dragonfly's soft, warm flesh. The wings roared like a jet engine, blasting air over them. They swooped lower between two towering skyscrapers before banking sharply into a ninety-degree turn. Snatchers swarmed around them, but the turbulence of the dragonfly's beating wings buffeted their flight paths into disarray. Kobi caught a reflection in a pane of glass on one of the buildings and saw himself clinging there, amazed.

They left the pursuing Snatchers in their wake and flew out over the bay. Kobi looked back toward the Space Needle. Several columns of smoke rose from the wreckage of the Observation Deck, where the number of drones was at last thinning. From the corner of his eye, he saw that three of the drones had split away and were preparing to charge at the dragonfly from directly below. Two were caught in the shifting air currents and veered off at angles, but the third kept coming, only jerking off course at the last moment. With a crash it collided with the dragonfly's wing.

The Snatcher plummeted like a rock, but the dragonfly's wing flailed. Kobi's stomach plunged as the giant insect listed in the air, then began to drop, its remaining wings losing their rhythm. For a few beats, it recovered before lurching downward again. Kobi clung on desperately, heartbeat ratcheting up at the impossibly huge drop below. Wind gusted in his ears as they lurched.

"We're going to crash!" bellowed Asha. "Hold on."

There was water below, then land as the dragonfly began to spin under the uneven thrust of its wings. The force threatened to rip Kobi and the others off. He leaned closer to the abdomen, gripping with knees and arms. It was the only thing he could do. Not that it was going to help. The ground was rushing up to meet them, buildings and trees and water in a blur. . . .

He didn't feel the impact. He only woke from unconsciousness, confused, body pulsing with pain. It could only have been a few seconds after the crash. He was lying on marshy grass, on his side, and he could hear groaning. Rolling over, he stared into a yellow eye the size of a basketball. The body of the dragonfly was bent horribly in two, its wings smashed beneath it.

"Asha?" he called.

It felt like his mind was rebooting and his body hadn't quite caught up. When he tried to stand, his legs gave way, and he fell back to his knees. There was a body a few yards away. It was Alan Apana. "Doctor?" he shouted.

"Kobi? Is that you?" The voice belonged to Yaeko, though he couldn't see her.

"Where are you?"

He stumbled over uneven ground, ankles sinking in mud. He heard a sound coming from the other side of the dead dragonfly, a rhythmic splashing like someone running toward him. He leaned against the insect's body for a moment, then peered over the top.

His heart almost stopped. A Snatcher was standing in the shallows, looming over Fionn, who was trying to crawl away.

"No!" Kobi cried. Somehow he managed to clamber over the abdomen and flopped down on the other side. But as he picked himself up, the Snatcher was already reaching down and scooping Fionn up. The younger boy began to scream. "No . . . ," Kobi said again, breaking into a sob.

A shadow passed over him, a hulking presence from behind. He heard the telltale chittering beep of a Snatcher. He turned and fell on his back, without even the strength to lift his arms. From beneath its metallic carapace, its stinger appeared, rearing back to strike at Kobi, the deadly toxin swirling in its capsule.

18

THE STINGER RETRACTED, AND the Snatcher's legs suddenly folded into its body as if it had deactivated. Kobi heard a rapid thumping sound, and a shadow passed overhead. *Helicopter?*

He twisted to see a large open-backed chopper land a few yards up the shoreline. The initials "CLAWS" were painted along the tail. Before its runners even hit the ground, rifle-carrying personnel in black hazmat suits jumped out. They approached the dragonfly with their weapons trained warily on it before the leader gave a number of hand signals. Kobi found himself staring into the barrel of a gun.

"Up!" said the man behind the visor.

Kobi did as he was told. All he got was a shove. Kobi grabbed the man's arms and flung him twenty feet. But others surrounded him, aiming their weapons. Fionn was being lifted over a soldier's shoulder, kicking and screaming. Kobi watched in horror as another soldier stepped over and struck Fionn's temple with the butt of his gun, knocking him out. Kobi searched frantically for the others and found them: Asha and Yaeko clung to each other as soldiers ushered them at gunpoint toward the helicopter's cargo doors. Apana was being practically dragged, struggling to stay upright. Once they were aboard the helicopter, the CLAWS guards lined them up on a single bench, then sat opposite, keeping their rifles raised. Fionn's head rolled weakly as the soldier dumped him in a seat and fastened the belt around his waist. Kobi still had a utility knife in his belt, but the hard faces behind the visors opposite told him it wouldn't be very smart to try and use it.

The helicopter took off, its nose swinging around in a wide arc before it surged forward in a gentle upward trajectory, evening out at a height well above even the tallest of the trees.

"*I'm sorry,*" said Fionn's voice. It sounded weak, and looking across, Kobi saw his eyes were only partially open.

"You saved our lives," said Asha. "You have nothing to apologize for."

"Yeah, you were amazing," added Yaeko.

Apana smiled at the soldiers opposite, a wide, beaming grin that turned to a grimace. "I guess the message got out, hey, fellas?" he said. The soldiers said nothing.

Kobi clung to that knowledge. His body felt stronger, already healed from the crash landing, and he tightened his fists in a surge of triumph. CLAWS had them. But the world must know the truth now. Relief spread through him, even as he knew they were heading to certain death at the hands of Melanie.

Kobi looked out of the side window as the old city flashed by. They were heading almost exactly due east, so he assumed they were being taken straight back to New Seattle, but the chopper began to descend again after only a few minutes. They passed over black water, and he suddenly knew exactly where they were going. A grand house came into view, surrounded by beautiful greenery. The helicopter hovered for a moment, then landed right in the middle of Alan Apana's yard. Another, smaller helicopter was already there.

The soldiers waited until the rotors stopped spinning before ordering Kobi and the others out onto the grass. Apana fell awkwardly to his knees, and Kobi helped him up. They huddled together right on the porch where Apana had smoked his cigar the night before.

The door to the veranda opened, and out stepped Melanie Garcia, holding a cocktail glass. She looked as immaculate as ever, dressed in a crisp gray suit and open-collared white shirt revealing her bony neck. Her gray bob had grown out and fell to her shoulders in glossy waves. She looked older than in the hologram Kobi encountered in the slums of New Seattle: her skin looked thin, almost stretched over her sharp, delicate cheekbones. Her expression was impassive: the only hint of human emotion lay in her hard eyes, glinting with satisfaction. Like a predator honing in on its injured prey. She was followed by a figure in a dress. It took Kobi a moment to place who it was. "*Niki!*" cried Asha.

Six months had transformed Niki completely. She'd grown taller, and her hair was different, piled on top of her head in a style fastened with a bright scarf, and she wore subtle makeup that accentuated her cheekbones. She looked so much older. She hitched her chin a fraction at the sight of them, but her eyes betrayed no joy at seeing her old friends.

"Hello, Alan," said Melanie, sipping her drink. "What a place you have here."

"You're too late," said Kobi. "We got the message out."

Melanie cocked her head. "Very resourceful of you," she said. "You've given our PR team a lot of work to do. Luckily we managed to black out most of the broadcast when we realized what was happening."

Was she bluffing? She spoke with such calm that Kobi began to doubt himself. Had it all been for nothing? He saw from the despair in the faces of the others that they believed her.

"Melanie," said Apana, speaking for the first time. "Think about it. We can start again."

Melanie chuckled to herself. "I've no wish to wind back that particular clock. You still don't get it even after all this time."

"Just take it yourself, then," said Apana. "Tell the world CLAWS has defeated the Waste. You can be a hero. There's a vial of pure, concentrated GAIA up in my lab. Just one drop can neutralize an area miles and miles in radius. You can save New Seattle."

"Do you really think we haven't had the GAIA 2.0 formula all this time?" Melanie asked. "Don't you remember? I was in charge of sending out the formula to our production labs." She shrugged. "I kept copies of all your files."

Despite all his treatment at the hands of CLAWS, Kobi still felt a rippling wave of shock stun him to the core. *They could have cleansed the Waste from the whole environment. All this time.*

"Melanie," pleaded Apana. "You're frightened, I know it. You didn't know what you were doing. All these years you've lived in terror of people finding out the truth. But, my dear, you must see sense now!"

"Do not patronize me, Alan!" said Melanie, her fingers tightening on the glass so hard Kobi thought it might shatter. "You think I'd let you endanger everything I've built? You're wrong."

"Melanie, dear," said Apana, suddenly sounding very old. "You can still fix things. You couldn't know the consequences of what you were planning. You are no scientist. It wasn't your fault."

Melanie's face flushed. "No! It was your fault!" she cried in a shrill voice. "Of course I didn't know what that formula would do—because *you* kept me out of everything. Favored Alex and Jonathan even after they turned down jobs with you. I should have listened when they told me you were too single-minded. You never valued me! Was it because I'm a woman? You thought I was weak, stupid. You didn't think I would ever defy you. You were going to fire me!"

"Melanie, you were like a daughter to me."

"You're a fraud, Alan. You use people. I might have released the Waste, but *you're* the one who's responsible."

Kobi started to understand the bitter resentment that burned in Melanie's eyes. Behind the cold, calculating exterior lay a need for recognition, a hatred of those who did not take her seriously, a need to destroy all others before she destroyed herself.

"I can't turn back now," said Melanie quietly, and for the briefest moment Kobi thought he could see the orphaned girl: lost, alone, abandoned, brilliant, terrified. "The path is set. Okay, let's finish this up." She spoke into a watch communicator. "Is it ready?"

A voice cracked back. "The device is in place. We're coming back now."

"What device?" said Kobi. A horrible feeling was creeping through his gut.

Melanie stared hard at him, unrelenting and devoid of any shred of empathy: the expression reminded Kobi of the analytical robotic eyes of a Snatcher. "You didn't think I'd come all the way out here just to say hi, did you, Kobi? Much as I trust our ability to spin your little message, we need to be sure the whole world knows who's responsible for the biggest terrorist attack in history."

"What are you talking about?" said Kobi.

"We've planted a little bomb," said Melanie. "Well, a big bomb, actually. Should be enough to wipe out most of this island. No one will ever know about these gardens or Apana. GAIA 2.0 will have never existed."

"You can't," said Apana. "An explosion that size will send Waste spores into the troposphere. Over the wall. They'll reach inhabited areas in—"

"For a genius, you can be very slow sometimes," said Melanie.

The truth slowly dawned on Kobi. "You *want* the Waste to spread. Even though millions will die. You'd do that just to keep control."

Melanie sighed. "No, *you* would."

"You're going to blame it on us?" said Asha.

"Yes, of course," said Melanie. "The world will believe Sol, the anarchist terrorist group, planted a bomb. They will do anything to destroy CLAWS. What better way than to target our global headquarters in New Seattle—a city CLAWS holds up as a symbol of their victory against the Waste? You can see their reasoning. Sol's last stand. Come on. The city is doomed anyway. The Sol agents we interrogated informed us of the Waste growth beneath New Seattle," said Melanie, sounding almost bored now. "I must admit, we never wanted quite that amount of Waste to find its way to the city. We underestimated its potency. Luckily, when the Waste overruns the city, we can blame you, and no one will ever presume that CLAWS failed to protect the citizens."

"Wow, you really are a sicko," said Yaeko. "Niki, are you hearing this? Tell me you're hearing this."

Niki just shook her head, not meeting her old friend's eye.

Yaeko threw out her hands. "Niki, I really think you should do something right about now. You're not a murderer. You think Melanie is your mother? She isn't. She is using you. You're just a commercial for CLAWS! Don't you get that?"

"Shut up, Yaeko!" yelled Niki, a surge of static electricity running over her fingertips.

"We're your family," said Fionn. "Not CLAWS."

"Ah, he speaks!" said Melanie. "Family. How heartwarming." She rounded on the kids. "You didn't see the world when the Waste struck. It was chaos. People trampling one another to get out of the city. Riots and looting." She shook her head in disgust. "CLAWS brought order again, but now that's crumbling. People need order. They need something to fear."

"You're wrong, Melanie," said Kobi. "People don't need you. You need them. Because you are weak. You think money and power will give you happiness. You have nothing."

"No!" snapped Melanie, throwing her glass into the side of the house, where it exploded. "You are only a boy. You don't understand a thing. They'll be cursing your name forever and the name of Sol and all you fugitives. History is what *I* decide."

She was practically spitting out the words as she spoke. Kobi knew that there was no way to convince Melanie. She could never be saved, but still Apana looked at her sadly. The CLAWS CEO gathered herself. "Time to go," she said.

"What are you going to do with us?" said Yaeko as the soldiers headed for the chopper.

"Nothing," said Melanie. "All you need to do is"—she pointed up—"smile." A drone was hovering above her head. On the side it read, "CLAWS NEWS." "Goodbye, fugitives."

She's leaving us here. . . .

Melanie nodded to the CLAWS soldiers, and they formed a line in front of her and Niki. Melanie walked toward the chopper.

"You can't do that!" shouted Niki. "You said we'd take them back!"

"Sorry, sweetheart," said Melanie. "But this has to be done. We have to protect the CLAWS brand. It is more important than any of us. It's the only thing that keeps the world together."

"But . . ." Niki looked distraught.

"No buts. We have to think of the greater good, dear. Remember what they are. Terrorists."

Yaeko snorted and shook her head contemptuously at Niki.

The soldiers filed back onto the chopper. *I need to do something*, thought Kobi. If he could overpower one, get a gun . . . somehow take out the others . . .

But the soldiers were well drilled, keeping him in their sights all the time as they settled in. The blades began to spin, and the helicopter rose off the ground.

Melanie strode toward the remaining smaller chopper and

climbed into the cockpit herself. "Come on, Niki, get in."

Niki didn't move from the veranda. She stared at Melanie across the yard, defiance in her eyes. "I'm not leaving without them," she said.

Melanie's gaze flickered with a trace of anger before her expression hardened. "Fine," she said. She slammed the cockpit door and began to manipulate the controls. The rotors spun.

"No! Wait!" cried Niki, running down the steps.

But Melanie's craft was already off the ground. Niki slowed as it rose higher above the house, then shot off to the east. Her shoulders slumped, and she turned to face Kobi and the others.

"Hey," said Yaeko. "At least you can die with a clean conscience, Nik." She went over and put her arm around the other girl.

"She said she'd keep you safe, Yaeko," said Niki. "I swear."

"You should have known you couldn't trust her," replied Asha. "After everything she's done."

"We need to get out of here before the bomb goes off," said Yaeko. As the helicopter flew away, Kobi noticed that a light had lit up on the news drone above them. He finally understood.

"No," he said.

"Um, yes," said Yaeko. "Fionn, could you call on a few of your friends to get us out?"

"I could try," said Fionn. "I could probably get a couple big enough to carry us." He closed his eyes as he projected the call.

"No," said Kobi. "We're not going to leave. We're going to try to stop that bomb. It's what Melanie wants us to do, but we have no choice."

Asha frowned. "What do you mean?"

Kobi stared up at the CLAWS News drone. "If they catch us near the bomb, it will look more like we are to blame. She'll turn the people trying to *save* the world into its destroyers. The same thing to Kobi that she did to Apana!"

"That's pretty clever," said Yaeko. Asha gave her a look, and Yaeko added, "What? It is. Nik, any way to stop that bomb?"

"I . . . I don't know," the girl said, still shaken.

"I have to try," said Kobi. "I have to."

"But that's what she wants!" said Fionn.

"I don't have a choice," replied Kobi. "I have to try to get it off the island into the lake."

"How will you find it?"

"It will be near the clonal spore sacs," said Apana. "That's where the highest concentration of Waste is, right at the epicenter of the GAIA 1.3 leak. It's at the center of the island. We passed it, Kobi—when I rescued you. Where the spores of the clonal organism are created."

Kobi began pacing toward the gate of the yard.

"Melanie planned for this, Kobi. You said it yourself," said Asha, rushing after him. "It must have some kind of lock on it or maybe a motion detector to stop you moving it."

"Sounds like Melanie," said Yaeko.

"But . . . I have to try," said Kobi. "I have to. You don't have long. Fionn, get everyone else out of here. Asha, make sure you use the cleansers right before the spores get to you."

Fionn shook his head, tears streaming from his eyes. *"No, Kobi."* He spoke through his telepathy, and Kobi sensed a wave of anguish.

"Do it! You guys are all that's left of Sol. You can't let it die today. Alan can help you get the truth out. But I have to do this. My dad gave everything to try to stop CLAWS—even his life. I have to do the same."

Asha gave him a long, despairing look. She rested a hand on Fionn's shoulder. "Do it, Fionn."

The boy tilted his face up at the sky with closed eyes, tears dripping from the corners. There were distant squawks, and two gigantic seagulls glided down, sweeping Kobi with a hurricane of wing beats as they flapped to slow themselves, thumping gnarled talons into the lawn in front of Apana's mansion. They both laid their huge wings flat against the grass, eyeing the five kids with a giant glassy stare.

"Go!" said Kobi.

Asha stepped toward him, but Kobi backed away, and with a final teary nod, Asha climbed onto one of the gulls.

"You get used to it," said Yaeko to Niki, who stared, horrified, at the gigantic beasts. One of them clacked its beak, and the other had its large black eyes fixed on Fionn.

The three kids climbed on, sitting in a line, gripping bunches of the birds' feathers. They helped pull Apana up. The old man looked frail. "Thank you for saving me," he said to Kobi. "And I don't just mean my life. Thank you for helping put right some of the things I did. Goodbye, Kobi Hales." They launched into the air.

Kobi watched them go and found himself smiling. He remembered the sweeping epic fantasy novels his father had read to him, where heroes would ride on the backs of magical birds. He almost laughed to think of what Hales's face would look like, seeing them all now. The branches of the trees in the yard bent under the blast of wind. As the great bird disappeared out of sight beyond the tall hedges he felt a strange, peaceful calm come over him.

"Kobi, if anything ever happens to me, you have to be brave. I won't always be here. When you're on your own, you still have to go on. That's the final rule."

As he heard his dad's familiar voice clear and strong in his mind, he turned and headed over the gravel path toward the end of the yard and the passage through the hedges. Above, the drone followed. It retreated high into the air—probably to keep the bomb from damaging it—until it became just a faint dot in the sky. Always watching.

Kobi ran into the tunnel cut into the hedges and felt the spray of the sprinklers wetting his face, his back, his legs. He wiped the water from his eyes. He reached the gate ahead, taking in the remarkable boundary between Waste and GAIA: the curling, decaying roots meeting the healing fertilizer and turning into bright beautiful flowers, healthy plants, large mushrooms, before falling away back into the deathly swamp. He stopped suddenly. An idea blazed through him. At first, he was too stunned to move. His whole body pulsed with a deep, desperate hope.

He turned and headed back toward the house.

19

HAVING LEFT THE YARD through the iron gate, Kobi charged through the constantly moving swampy morass of the clonal organism, dodging trees that shot up all around, leaping over cracks and bulging roots as the ground expanded and shifted beneath his feet. He squinted against the thick cloud of spores stinging his eyes, streaming down his throat. The voices infiltrated his mind again, but this time they weren't so welcoming: Kobi could tell they sensed the intention in his mind. The clonal organism knew he meant to destroy it.

What are you doing? Do not do this! Leave!

The ground to his left stirred as a pale tendril broke the surface and snaked toward him. Kobi rolled away, then managed to get to his feet.

We don't want you here. . . . We will consume you!

He dodged quickly as more roots tried to claim him. The mist thickened. He wasn't sure of distance at all. One of his feet slipped on a patch of fungus, and a cloud of spores burst around his body. He flailed his arms to clear a path, staggering. He felt unmoored from his own limbs, dizzy to the point he could barely walk at all, and his conscious mind told him this had been a terrible mistake. A creeping, insidious fear clenched at his heart like an icy fist. He should have listened to Asha and the others. If he had, they could all be flying to safety this very minute.

He stared around in increasing panic, blinking, searching for the bomb. How would he even spot it?

Something snagged his foot and quickly dragged him to his knees. Pressure tightened around his calf, and he was tugged violently facedown through the muck. Rancid swamp water filled his mouth. He spat it out. *I have to get free!* He turned over, grabbed the vine between his hands, and twisted hard. It loosened enough for him to get away. Kobi jumped to his feet and ran, splashing between the fungi. How far had he come? Half a mile? How long did he have left to go?

Then he saw it. Red lights flashing through the gray. He dashed toward it. The bomb was the size of his entire bed back in the Sol base but sleek, like a black lozenge of metal. He ran his hands across the surface, looking for any hatch, a sign of wiring. He'd helped Hales wire up mines connected to trip wires to use as base defenses—there was always a safety wire to defuse the explosives. But there was nothing on this device. He didn't dare move it. He guessed Asha must be right: there probably was a movement sensor that would set it off if Kobi tried to move it. If he even could. Above, he was aware of the CLAWS news drone filming him as he crouched over the bomb, assembling second by second of incriminating footage that would paint him as a villain as bad as Apana.

How long did he have? There was no timer on the bomb, not like in the old movies he'd watched with his dad, and with Rohan and Leon at the Sol base, wiling away time; the old action movies where all you had to do was pull out one of the wires and the bomb would deactivate. If only it was that easy. Kobi knew the bomb could go off any second.

Please, just a little longer. Give me a little longer.

He took out the vial. The green liquid inside the glass tube swilled in the container. The extract of pure concentrated GAIA 2.0 that he'd run and taken from Apana's loft.

What now? Smash it over the ground, then simply wait? What if the blast incinerated the GAIA compound before it could take effect?

"This way, Kobi. . . ."

Kobi looked up, reeling and nauseous, because that wasn't the voice of the clonal organism but a different, familiar tone. And when he saw Jonathan Hales standing just a few yards away, it made no sense at all. It couldn't be him because Hales was dead, and this version of Hales was young, healthy, wearing his gym tracksuit from back at Bill Gates. A whistle hung on a chain around his neck.

"You're doing well, Kobi," he said. "Just a little bit farther."

"Dad?" said Kobi.

Hales smiled and wagged a finger. "No slacking, now. Stick with it."

Kobi moved toward him, but Hales turned and drifted deeper into the mist between twisted trees, their branches coated in bulbous fungal growths. Somewhere beneath the heady confusion suffocating his brain, Kobi knew this must be a hallucination. But it seemed so real.

"Dad! Wait!" said Kobi. He could barely see, barely even breathe. The air seemed thick as tar. He was beginning to panic when he saw Hales waiting by a massive knotted trunk of barkless wood. Its branches rose almost out of sight above, where they spread and drooped like arachnid legs that reached back into the earth, rooting themselves there. He knew instinctively he was looking at the heart of the clonal organism, the center of this massive amalgamation of Waste-infected life.

"This is where it ends, Kobi," said Hales.

The ground trembled, and more vines broke through, their tips rising like bony fingers, defying gravity. One looped around his chest and another across his shoulders. He managed to rip the first away, but others had already latched on. They squeezed Kobi slowly and forcefully and unstoppably, like a vise, pulling him toward the trunk of the tree, pressing his back into the wood. A root tickled his neck, skidding gently across his skin. He fought, jerking this way and that, but they weren't giving up their hold. Each of his limbs was snared by what felt like bands of steel, cutting into his muscles and keeping his arms trapped against the trunk.

Hales, untethered, walked in front on him. He looked calm.

"Dad! Help me!"

"Almost done now, son. It's almost over. You know what to do. Time to end this."

And in that moment, Kobi understood. With the vial still in his hand and only able to move a fraction, he crushed the glass against the trunk, feeling the shards cut into his hand. His blood and the GAIA liquid mingled and trickled to the ground, disappearing into the black earth.

What now? The roots against his neck were cutting off his air flow.

"Dad . . . ," he wheezed. Hales was looking down.

By Kobi's feet, a hint of green. Kobi's gaze fell on a tiny shoot rising delicately, exploring the air. Not the clonal organism but something pure. Life emerging, just as his own was about to end.

Jonathan Hales reached out a hand and stroked his cheek.

"You did it, son. You—"

A deafening boom ripped the world to pieces.

EPILOGUE

AT BIG EARL'S DINER in New York City, Johanna pushed away an uneaten plate of pancakes. She was wearing glasses, and the putty on her face was uncomfortable. Her escape from the Sol base with a few others had been lucky. Spike had used his drone bug to disable Snatchers as he, Johanna, Mischik, and a few others had fled through the sewers out into the slums. Mischik's contacts had gotten them out of New Seattle, smuggled them onto a train headed east. Now, across from Johanna at the table, Mischik—wearing a wig—was checking the internet for more stories questioning CLAWS. "The Revolution has begun," he'd said.

Too bad it was too late for Kobi and the others, Johanna thought as she glanced down at the large photo of Kobi in the newspaper. It was a feature piece from the *New York Times* running through Kobi's story. And fortunately, the staff at the paper did not buy official statements from CLAWS.

Almost two weeks had passed since the pirate broadcast from Old Seattle: Kobi and the man the world thought was dead standing in a lush garden with their story of the truth behind the Waste disaster, the accusations against Melanie Garcia. The evil with which CLAWS had deceived the world, experimented on children, held back a way to prevent the suffering of millions. The story had caused quite a stir in the slums and some riots that CLAWS quickly quashed.

The denials had been quick and featured on every channel. The CLAWS spokespeople vehemently denied what they called baseless claims, calling the pirate broadcast "terrorist propaganda" and a last-ditch effort by Sol to destabilize the government after the successful assault on their hideout. Apana, they stated, was the true terrorist ringleader and always had been, operating a cell from his base in the old city itself and plotting to overwhelm New Seattle with the same deadly contagion as twenty years before.

The bomb, according to their story, was proof that Apana was a terrorist—detonated as brave CLAWS security personnel had closed in on his island fortress and center of operations. Drone footage showed Kobi near the bomb before it activated, and the aftermath: a great black cloud hanging over the familiar skyline of the old city, and on the ground, a huge crater in the middle of the black expanse of Mercer Island. The boy called Kobi Hales, Alan Apana, and the rest of the child fugitives had all been killed in the suicide attack.

In the days afterward all of New Seattle was on edge. There was no doubt, scientists warned, that the explosion would have sent Waste spores high into the atmosphere. It was a matter of time and chance where they would spread, but CLAWS had vowed to be vigilant and ready to react with emergency medical care when it was needed. New Seattle was evacuated, but not everyone could get out in time. Melanie Garcia herself had come onto the nightly news shows, her face pale, eyes dark from lack of sleep. "We're working around the clock," she said. "There will be casualties, that much is certain, but we ask the people of New Seattle and around the world to trust us. Together we're stronger than these heartless monsters. We beat the Waste before. We can do it again."

Johanna's blood had boiled with rage.

Over the coming days, though, the anger changed to determination. The world had settled back into normal life. Johanna heard snatches of conversation that raised her spirits. People spoke about the truth of Kobi and Apana's claim: why would Apana appear after all this time just to lie? Why would children be used to plant the bomb? Where had Niki, the poster girl of CLAWS drugs, gone? Were her mutations part of the same experiments Kobi had talked about? There was word of Horizon, a one-hundred-percent-effective cleanser—now lost, thanks to CLAWS. News articles appeared that called GAIA 2.0 a myth that appealed only to the gullible. But in other forums online and across social media, people were questioning CLAWS. The president had ordered the launch of an investigation.

Johanna had started volunteering at a Waste clinic in Queens for those showing signs of contamination spreading from the Wastelands in agricultural parts of New York State. She was staying with the family of the head doctor there. Only if her colleagues and patients looked very closely would they see she wasn't one of them, that her fingertips were slightly elongated, her nails tinged faintly green. As long as she didn't use her powers ostentatiously, staying hidden wasn't all that hard.

She grieved for her friends. She missed them terribly, and guilt plagued her waking thoughts and her dreams, robbing her of her appetite, bringing her at sudden moments to tears. Perhaps if she had gone with the other Wastelings, things might have turned out different.

Johanna left her seat and went to the counter to pay. She was due at the clinic in ten minutes for another shift. So far there were no indications of increased Waste infections, but everyone was on tenterhooks. She was handing over her credits when the door slammed open. All the customers looked up. It was a man in construction clothes.

"Hey, what's up, Ed?" said the server. "I know the coffee's good here, but—"

"Turn on the news!" shouted the man, pointing at the holo-display above the counter. "Haven't you seen?"

The server scrambled for the remote and brought up a news channel. The display above the anchor read, "Breaking News," and across the bottom of the screen a headline flashed.

THE END OF THE WASTE?

A feed beneath rolled past with a series of subheads.

". . . story is still developing," said the anchor, "but initial indications are that we have an unexpected environmental incident in

Old Seattle." She touched her earpiece. "Okay, we have live images of the scene coming from our news drone over the old city. . . ." She disappeared, replaced with footage filmed from several hundred feet above the Seattle Wastelands. Johanna saw the towering wall separating the old city. But something had changed. For instead of the black expanse of fire-scoured earth outside, the landscape was vibrant green. The camera panned out, showing the spread of the new vegetation. It reached for miles: trees—not mutated but regular-size oaks, birches, larches, ferns, hollies—and meadows of flowers and grassland; lush, delicate plants unlike the towering thick roots and billowing giant waxy petals that designated Waste-mutated life.

"I'm not sure what we're seeing," said the anchor's voice-over. "How is that even possible? All we know from drone testing is that the new growth is not caused by Waste."

"It's GAIA," Johanna whispered. "They did it. How?"

Mischik was staring at the screen, standing up, a look of utter amazement on his face. "The spores that were blown out of the city . . . they weren't carrying Waste. They carried GAIA." Thoughts flickered across his twitching features, and he was muttering fervently to himself. "They somehow administered the real, working GAIA to the plant life before it was decimated. It's the only way. Kobi, you genius!"

A few people turned to look at him before focusing on the holo-display again.

"There was life beneath the scorched lands ready to be awoken," said Johanna. "Forest fires rejuvenate ecologies; they don't destroy them. The Scorchers left plenty of seeds and plants alive beneath the sand, fertile and waiting to be given a spurt of life."

The drone descended, swooping low over the new growth. The diner watched in silence.

". . . we go now to CLAWS headquarters and an interview with Director Melanie Garcia."

Melanie appeared on the display in front of the skyscraper that housed Healhome, with several microphones aimed in her direction.

"Melanie, has CLAWS had knowledge of the existence of GAIA for years? Are you responsible for the continuing threat of Waste? Do you have on your hands the blood of millions of lives that could have been saved?"

Melanie's face was taut and anxious. She spoke weakly, reciting prepared words. "It's far too early to say what we're seeing—this could be a new mutation of the Waste, and we must take every precaution to ensure that it doesn't reach New Seattle. I'll be convening with our crisis team in the next hour, and we plan to mobilize our incinerator drones to tackle the threat."

"Perhaps you haven't heard," said a reporter. "Several cities to the south are reporting enhanced crop growth of healthy Waste-free plants. It looks like whatever escaped Old Seattle is actually beneficial. People are saying GAIA 2.0 is real. Government scientists have corroborated it."

"I'd urge people to be cautious in their suppositions," said

Melanie Garcia. "More tests will need to be—"

The footage switched back to the news anchor. "I'm sorry to interrupt the interview, but I'm hearing we have more breaking news. We are receiving a transmission from within Old Seattle itself."

The image that came up on-screen made Johanna gasp, and her heart soared. It was Kobi. He was standing on what looked like an indoor basketball court, though the walls and the rim and backboard were each covered in a layer of vines and leaves. "Is it working?" he said to someone out of frame. "Are we transmitting?"

"Yes, you are!" whispered Johanna.

Kobi nodded and smiled. "I hope you can see me," he said. "It took a while to put this together. My name is Kobi Hales, and whatever CLAWS tells you, I'm alive. We're alive." He beckoned with his hand. "Come on, guys, show them." Tears sprang into Johanna's eyes as others walked into view—Asha, Fionn, Yaeko, and—was that?—Niki! They were all grinning as they crowded in next to Kobi, who continued speaking in a serious voice. "CLAWS tried to silence us with their bomb," he said, "but we survived. And right now GAIA 2.0 is spreading across Old Seattle—neutralizing the Waste in the mutated wildlife. It may even have reached you too, wherever you're watching this. My friends here used to have to take cleansers, but we've been living clean for days. The air is healthy again." He paused. "I know this will be hard for you to believe, because for years CLAWS has fed you lies, but soon you won't need them anymore. Their tyranny is over." He raised his fist. "Long live GAIA! Okay, that should do it." He approached the camera, reached across in front of it, and the footage ended abruptly.

The news anchor returned, touching her earpiece and looking confused. "We're still digesting this with you, folks, so bear with us. I think we need to return to CLAWS HQ and see what they make of the latest developments."

Melanie was talking to a colleague, then turned abruptly and marched up the steps into the CLAWS building, followed by a barrage of shouted questions. The CLAWS representative she'd left behind bent toward the microphones. "We have no comment at this time." Then he too scurried inside.

"Long live GAIA!" said Johanna, laughing.

"You think that was okay?" asked Kobi.

"It was perfect!" Niki replied.

"You're a natural," said Asha, grinning.

The decommissioned Snatcher sat on the gym floor, trailing wires where they'd opened up its recording hardware to send their message.

"So what now?" said Yaeko.

"I think we just wait," said Kobi. "Once GAIA spreads, the world will come to us."

"How long will that take?" asked Niki.

Kobi shrugged. "I've no idea."

Asha grabbed a baseball mitt and ball from the side of the

room. "Let's have a game to celebrate. Been a while since Team Wasteling practiced."

Kobi smiled. "I wish Rohan was here to see this. But there's something I have to do before playing."

"Mysterious," said Asha, cocking her eyebrow. "We'll be outside."

Leaving the Snatcher dormant on the basketball court, Kobi walked through the overgrown corridors of Bill Gates High School. It already seemed smaller than the last time he'd been here, classrooms and hallways completely overrun with plant life. In their dorm, Kobi had found his old bed, their camping stove, their shelves of books, all buried under shrubs. They'd spent a day just cutting back the growth, hacking trails through the thickets.

He still couldn't believe he'd made it back to the school at all. Ten days earlier, he'd woken half submerged in mud and lay there for what could have been hours, trying to piece together what had happened. He couldn't hear anything but a dull ringing. Slowly, the fragments of his memory locked together, and he remembered the bomb. His injuries were severe. As well as what he guessed were perforated eardrums, he'd had burns across his face and chest. Where his clothes had burned away, his skin was scabbed and bruised in shades of purple and angry red. His left arm wouldn't move at all, and both his legs screamed in pain with even the smallest shift of his body. For at least a day and a night he'd drifted in and out of consciousness, hungry and thirsty, but every time he woke, he felt stronger.

As he woke to a dawn sky one day, he realized he wasn't alone. A giant gull stood nearby, Fionn and Asha on its back.

"Is this a dream?" he'd said. "Are you real?"

"*That should be my question*," said Fionn. "*Asha sensed you were still alive.*"

The pain as they wrestled him onto the eagle told him he definitely wasn't dreaming, and he passed out again. When he woke, they were already landing at the high school, where Yaeko and Niki were waiting to help him inside.

For the first two days after, he'd done nothing but rest. On the third day he could walk with a stick, and by the seventh he barely had a limp. He wasn't sure how he'd survived the bomb at all. Maybe the trunk of the gnarled Waste tree had shielded him from the worst of the concussive blast. But that seemed impossible. Secretly Kobi thought he knew the answer: it couldn't be explained by science, not totally. He remembered the spirit of Jonathan Hales watching over his body. His dad had protected him. Not literally. It was something he had given Kobi, something inside him.

Johanna had told Kobi, back at the Sol base all those weeks ago: *Our powers run far deeper, and are more complex than we know. Our powers depend on our state of mind, on our physiology—on something inside. It's different for all of us. You have to find that thing inside you.*

Kobi had found it: something inside him so strong his body had survived the central blast zone of the bomb.

Kobi made his way past the gym, through the showers, and into the changing room: none of those had escaped the encroaching vegetation, and a filigree of vines covered the lockers, with springy moss on the floor. The locker room was where his whole journey had begun six months ago, when he'd set out alone to find the man he thought was his father. He paused with his hand on locker D22 and drew a breath to steady himself. Several times since coming back he'd thought about opening it, but something—fear, perhaps?—had made him reluctant. He wasn't sure he was ready now, but he exhaled and pulled open the locker door.

"Hey, Max," he said, addressing the boy in the photo tacked to the inside of the door. "Long time no see."

Maxwell Trenton, whose name was inside every book within, had been the owner of the locker before the Waste hit. A short kid, chubby, with a crooked smile, he looked maybe twelve from the photo, taken with two members of the Seattle Seahawks NFL team.

There was only one book inside the locker now, under a Seahawks cap. Kobi took it out carefully. The Yearbook, with the annual photos Hales had taken of them both. Kobi flicked through from the earliest, when he was just a baby in Hales's arms, through his toddlerhood, then as gap-toothed young boy. For every year that Kobi aged, Hales seemed to age five, turning from an athletic young man to a hunched elderly one as the Waste wreaked havoc on his metabolism. It was a stark reminder of the price he had paid for keeping Kobi safe. The only thing that remained the same in each photo was the look on Hales's face. Pride, protectiveness, a hint, at the edges of the eyes, of fear.

Love.

Kobi slid the last picture from his back pocket—charred around the edges—into the Yearbook and placed the Yearbook back in the locker.

"Bye, Dad," he said, closing the door gently. "I love you too."

Fionn's panicking voice punctured his thoughts. *"Kobi—quickly! Get out here!"*

Kobi ran from the locker room and down the hall, leaping vines and roots and pushing leaves aside. As he burst through the school's front doors he saw the Snatchers had already arrived. Dozens of them hovered over the school, and more landed on the ground, completely encircling the Wastelings with their stingers poised.

"How did they find us so fast?" asked Yaeko.

The *wup-wup* sound of rotors approached, and over the trees three helicopters appeared. Not CLAWS but military. They landed on the old school field, and the soldiers jumped out in camouflage fatigues, wearing visored helmets and clutching their weapons. In single file they ran up the bank toward where Kobi and his friends were pinned back by the Snatchers.

The lead soldier swiped over his wrist tablet. Instantly the Snatchers on the ground lowered their stingers and shut down. The ones in the air shot off vertically, then flew over the school and out of sight.

"You're not CLAWS?" said Asha.

"We're not," said the sergeant, lifting his visor.

"But the Snatchers—"

"CLAWS doesn't control them anymore. They don't control much at all, actually. Is this all of you? The Sol kids?"

Kobi looked at his four companions. "That's right. Who are you?"

"Federal response team," said the soldier. "Monitoring the new growth. We traced your broadcast signal. You can't stay here—important people need to talk with you. The president, for one. But hey—there's a hero's welcome waiting for you at home."

Home . . . , thought Kobi. It seemed an odd choice of word. What was home if not this place, where he'd lived most of his life?

He and his friends looked at one another. He'd always known they'd be leaving at some point, he supposed. Only Fionn looked upset at the thought, and Asha hugged him close, whispering to him. He sniffed and nodded.

"We need to make another stop," said Kobi to the soldier. "Alan Apana needs a ride."

The soldier's eyes went wide. "Apana is alive? Sorry, I thought he hadn't made it. Where is he?"

Kobi shook his head. "Looking after his strawberry bushes. He's got a bunker at his mansion on Mercer Island. The whole house got destroyed in the bomb blast, but there's a greenhouse in the bunker, and he wanted to save the last of his fruits and vegetables. Guess when you live with nothing but plants for thirteen years, you get kind of attached to them."

"Right," said the soldier. "I guess we'll need to stop off there, then." He frowned. "Strawberry bushes?"

Kobi smiled as the soldier relayed the destination to the pilot through his radio. Kobi knew it wasn't just his produce Apana was going back for. The emergency bunker was meant to be an emergency fallout shelter in case anyone ever decided to blow up the Wasteland. It contained personal mementos, photos of his family, his son's old guitar. The room and its contents were all that was left of his home, and he needed to say goodbye to it. Kobi understood the feeling.

The Wastelings followed the troops down toward the helicopters and climbed on board the largest. Soon Bill Gates High School was falling away beneath them.

"You said CLAWS wasn't in charge anymore!" Kobi shouted over the blades' roar.

"There are warrants out for the arrest of Melanie Garcia and the rest of the board," said the sergeant. "Their assets are frozen pending a federal investigation."

Kobi should have felt a thrill of triumph at the thought of Melanie going to jail, but he took the news with barely a flicker of joy. What did it matter now? As long as CLAWS was out of the picture, that was enough.

"Where are you taking us?" he asked.

"The CLAWS medical program has been suspended and turned over to us." He looked askance at Kobi. "Is it really true your blood made those cleansers? We tested the Horizon. It is incredible. It's a two-pronged attack: we cleanse anyone who's already infected, and GAIA makes sure they'll never get recontaminated. You really are the savior, you know that?"

Kobi grinned. "People keep trying to call me that."

The soldier whistled. "They'll want to keep you in a layer of Bubble Wrap!"

Kobi felt uneasy at the thought but laughed it off. He'd be back to being prodded at and examined, his blood taken and analyzed. But that was his duty, and compared with the fates of so many others who'd fought CLAWS and the Waste, it was a light one.

Asha was watching him from across the other side of the chopper, smiling warmly.

"You'll be fine," she said. "You're not on your own anymore."

Kobi thought of Jonathan Hales. He'd known from the start how special Kobi was and what he represented. And everything he'd done had been designed to keep Kobi safe, even if it meant giving his own life. Kobi couldn't let that sacrifice be in vain.

Below they crossed the wall, and the green expanse seemed to stretch forever.

"I was never alone," he replied.